Also by Terry Davis

Vision Quest

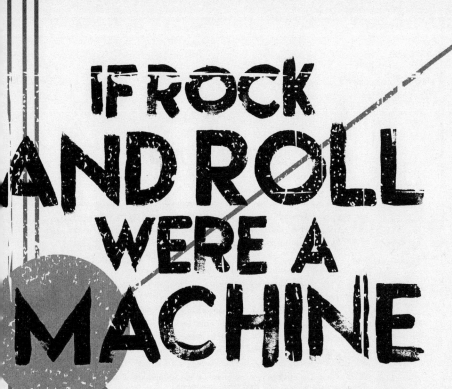

IF ROCK AND ROLL WERE A MACHINE

TERRY DAVIS

SIMON & SCHUSTER BFYR

New York London Toronto Sydney New Delhi

An imprint of Simon & Schuster Children's Publishing Division
1230 Avenue of the Americas, New York, New York 10020
This book is a work of fiction. Any references to historical events, real people,
or real places are used fictitiously. Other names, characters, places, and events
are products of the author's imagination, and any resemblance to actual events
or places or persons, living or dead, is entirely coincidental.
Text copyright © 1992 by Terry Davis
Originally published in 1992 by Delacorte Press
Cover illustration copyright © 2015 by Nick Yarger
All rights reserved, including the right of reproduction in whole or in part in any form.
SIMON & SCHUSTER BFYR is a trademark of Simon & Schuster, Inc.
For information about special discounts for bulk purchases, please contact Simon & Schuster
Special Sales at 1-866-506-1949 or business@simonandschuster.com.
The Simon & Schuster Speakers Bureau can bring authors to your live event. For more
information or to book an event, contact the Simon & Schuster Speakers Bureau at
1-866-248-3049 or visit our website at www.simonspeakers.com.
Also available in a SIMON & SCHUSTER BFYR hardcover edition
Cover design by Lizzy Bromley; interior design by Tom Daly
The text for this book is set in Perpetua Std.
Manufactured in the United States of America
2 4 6 8 10 9 7 5 3 1
CIP data for this book is available from the Library of Congress.
ISBN 978-1-4814-5633-3 (hc)
ISBN 978-1-4814-5632-6 (pbk)
ISBN 978-1-4814-5634-0 (eBook)

To all the teachers and coaches

who were kind to me

Contents

. . . I say live it out like a god

Sure of immortal life, though you are in doubt,

Is the way to live it.

If that doesn't make God proud of you

Then God is nothing but gravitation,

Or sleep is the golden goal.

—"David Matlock"
from Edgar Lee Master's,
Spoon River Anthology

"...Though much is taken, much abides...

Some work of noble note may yet be done."

—Alfred, Lord Tennyson,
Ulysses, 1842

Acknowledgments

I'm not exaggerating when I say the following teachers and coaches and the one neighborhood dad helped save my life. There's nothing in the world that lifts a kid's spirit like a smile on the face of an adult when he or she sees you coming. If these good people are happy to see you, you can't be as worthless as you feel.

My children and I owe the following people a debt of the heart. I was just another young human being to them, but to me they are the exceptions that shaped the man I try every day to become.

Everywhere Spirit, Bless these souls and the ones I've forgotten.

Mrs. Bockmeyer
Don Cobb
Pat Coontz
Gary Davis
Maxine Dicus
Joe Heslin
Dick Hoover
John Irving
Gene Kelly

Barry Livengood
Pat McManus
Barney Overlie
Cecil Robinette
Nick Scarpelli
Ted Solotaroff
Bill Via
Bill Waddington

Chapter 1

Albert Bowden Gives His Word

Bert Bowden is having trouble with the essay.
Class is already half over and he's gone through three introductory paragraphs on three different subjects. The topic Tanneran assigned was "The Worst Thing That Ever Happened to Me," and Bert said under his breath, "Oh, boy. Have I got material for this." But that is turning out to be the problem: Bert can't choose from among all the shitty things that have happened to him in his sixteen, almost seventeen, years. And now he can't concentrate because his mind is full of the awareness that he's living through another one of those things right now.

It's the first day of Bert's junior year, he's got the guy everybody says is the best English teacher in school, English is the only class he likes, and now he's going to flunk the first in-class essay because he can't focus.

Bert dug into the assignment right away. His grandfather was placed in a rest home last spring, and the old man is always on his mind. Before he finished the introduction, though, Bert realized this wasn't the worst thing that ever happened to him. It hadn't happened to him. Bert wasn't the one who suffered the embarrassment of having to be cleaned up like a baby. Bert wasn't the one "living," as his parents referred to his grandfather's condition, in the "home," as they called the place. This is not the worst thing that ever happened to you, Bert thought. This is the worst thing that ever happened to Gramp. And he flipped the sheet in his ring binder and started again.

When sincerity didn't work, Bert turned to sarcasm. He assumed the voice of an indignant teenager, which he is to a degree, and began describing the 1969 Harley-Davidson Sportster that sits in the window of Shepard's Classic and Custom Cycles. His parents won't let him buy it, even though he has the money in the bank. "Motorcycles are too dangerous" is what his father says, and "That money is for college" is his mother's response. Bert doesn't have the grades to get into any college worth going to. So since he can't get into a decent college and faces a bleak future, anyway, he might as well have fun and die young on a beautiful old Harley. But Bert is tired of being sarcastic. He got by on sarcasm and humor in his essays last year, and he doesn't want to be funny now. He wants to be serious. Don't be a wiseass, Bert told himself. Don't resort to that cheap crap anymore. And he flipped the sheet.

Bert thought and thought: What was the worst thing that ever happened to him?

Tanneran looked like he'd been an athlete when he was younger. Maybe he'd be impressed by Bert's bad luck in sports last year. So Bert began writing about getting mononucleosis and missing varsity baseball tryouts. He entitled it "Mononuked." But he scratched it out. It was just more of that cute shit he always resorted to. Besides, there wasn't a chance in the world he'd have made varsity his sophomore year. And this made him think that maybe the worst thing that ever happened to him was going to a high school with twenty-four hundred students where it was incredibly tough to make the teams, and how if he lived in a smaller town he'd not only make all the teams but probably be a star.

But then he realized this was just more shit. I have to be who I am, he thought, but I don't have to lie to myself or other people to make me feel better about it. So he flipped the sheet.

And now he looks up at the clock and sees that junior English is over for today. He sees that Tanneran is looking too. The man turns to face the class. "Time's up," he says. "That's all, folks. Make sure your names are on 'em."

The bell rings, kids rise, voices rise, the youth of America stride forward into the circular flow of another school year.

But Bert Bowden remains seated, writing his name slowly. He will submit this blank sheet. He will add a paper to the pile like everyone else.

Tanneran is sitting on his desk, the pile of papers in his hand, as Bert slides his on top. "I wrote three different introductory paragraphs, but nothing worked," Bert says. "I want to do the assignment. Can I bring it in tomorrow, Mr. Tanneran?"

Tanneran looks back down at the paper. "Albert Bowden," he says.

"Actually, I go by Bert," Bert says. "I just thought I'd present myself formally since myself was all I had to present."

Tanneran smiles. "Not a bad move in desperation." He stands and walks toward the door. Bert follows.

"Tell you what, Bert," Tanneran says in the doorway. "You give me your word you'll submit an essay tomorrow at the start of class?"

"I give you my word," Bert replies.

Chapter 2

Parting Ways

It's only the first week of school, but it's the third week of football practice. Two-a-days are over, the timed miles are over. The coaches are pretty sure by now who the real players are, but there's still the final cut to be made. They don't spend a lot of time conditioning. They warm up, drill, and scrimmage.

Warm-ups are over now and the team has broken down by position. Linemen work at one end of the field, backs and ends at the other. Bert is one of four quarterbacks throwing passes to a line of receivers. He crouches with the ball in his hands over the imaginary center, listens as backfield coach Joe Heslin says "Post" in a conversational tone, scans the imaginary defense, does not look at the receiver, calls out in his most commanding voice "Hut! Hut! Hut!," and on that third sound turns and drops back deep into the imaginary pocket where he sets up and throws to Camille Shepard, who has head-faked the imaginary defender and cut toward the goalpost. The ball floats out fat and sweet, revolving slowly enough for Shepard to count the laces. It's a little short, though. But Shepard reaches back with his left hand and pulls it in.

Bert doesn't look too bad. Until you see the other quarterbacks, that is.

Sean Christman, a junior who played a little on the varsity team last year, is next to take the ball from Coach Heslin. Christman is six feet two inches tall, five inches taller than Bert, and weighs two hundred pounds to Bert's one-sixty. Christman calls out the count in a voice like the drill sergeant from *Full Metal Jacket*, drops back and bullets the ball to a sophomore running a hook. The kid turns and the ball is there. It hits him in the numbers before he can get his hands up. The kid rubs his chest as he trots back to the receiver line. Bad move, Bert thinks. Dropping the ball is no big deal, but rubbing the hurt is a bad, bad move.

Compared to Sean Christman, Bert sounds and looks like a little boy. But Christman is only the number two quarterback.

As Bert watches Mike Jackson, Thompson's first-team QB for the past two years, step up to throw, he wonders if Christman ever wishes he went to another school. He must. He'd be first-team at any other school in the city. But his dad is Thompson's head football coach and they live in the Thompson district. It wouldn't look good for the coach's son to transfer out of district so he could be starting quarterback at another school.

Bert thinks how lame it is for him to wish he went to a smaller school so he could make first team in everything and have a chance to stand out, when a really excellent athlete like Christman is stuck behind a great athlete like Jackson.

Bert thinks about Camille Shepard. He's heard that Shepard came to the States from France to spend the year with his father, the owner of Shepard's Classic and Custom. He pronounces his name "Cam-ee," but a lot of the guys and all the coaches except Heslin still call him "Cam-eel," which is how Coach Christman pronounced it when he read it off the list on the first day of practice. His black hair comes down past his shoulders, and he rides a Harley. He's bigger than Sean Christman and he's not effeminate, so calling him a girl's name rings particularly stupid to Bert.

Camille's dad, who also rides a Harley, had been watching the practices until one day another biker, an outlaw-looking guy on a louder bike, showed up with him. Coach Christman turned to look when he heard the roar. Practice stopped as he watched the two men pull into the parking lot, shut off their bikes, and amble toward the field. He met them at the edge of the running track, spoke something Bert couldn't hear, and pointed back toward the bikes.

The outlaw, who was the same height as both Shepards but slimmer and whose arm muscles reminded Bert of those rawhide knots people buy for their dogs to chew on, got right in Christman's face. Everybody sprinted in around them.

Coach Heslin told Bert to run across the street to any house and call 911.

A patrol car came howling through the parking lot as

Bert was running back across the street. There was no fight, and Bert wouldn't have wanted to see one. But he was disappointed to have missed the heated conversation.

Camille tried to go with them when the cops walked his dad and the outlaw to their car, but his dad wouldn't let him.

Nobody could believe it when they saw the cops search the outlaw biker and find a gun in a shoulder holster. They put him and Shepard into the back of the car, then one of them read their IDs into the radio.

Coach Christman yelled for everybody to get back to work, but no one, including the other coaches, was in a hurry to do it.

When the one cop put the mike down, both he and his partner climbed out of the car and opened the back doors for Shepard and the outlaw. They returned the gun, then the four men shook hands all around.

Bert caught the expression of disgust on Christman's face before he blew his whistle and turned away. Even wearing his helmet and with all the noises of practice Bert heard the rumble of the outlaw's Harley a long way into the distance.

Bert wonders what it was like for Camille Shepard to grow up thousands of miles from his father. He also wonders if life had given him the choice, whether he would have traded growing up with his parents in a normal home—if you can call growing up without any brothers and sisters normal—for the body and athletic ability of a guy like Camille. If life would have thrown in the Harley, Bert would have traded.

Thinking about a guy of another nationality makes Bert think about the subject of race, and Bert is wondering if Christman resents being second-team to a black kid more than he would to a white kid, when he becomes aware of silence. Bert's vision registers movement and the color brown right before he takes a whack in his face mask. The ball bounces at his feet, and he moves as fast as he can to pick it up.

Heslin's voice is the first sound Bert realizes he has heard for a while. He looks at the big gray-haired man, the oldest of the coaches. "Feel all right, Bowden?" Heslin asks. "Looked like you lost consciousness there."

"I'm okay," Bert says.

Heslin waves his hand toward the imaginary line of scrimmage. "Then let's get back to work," he says.

Bert's mind is full of white noise—like a stereo speaker turned up full blast when the station has gone off the air— as he bends his knees and holds his hands out as though to receive the snap. He doesn't hear what pattern Heslin has called, but he begins the count, anyway. "Hut! Hut! Hut!"

Kelly McDougall, last year's starting wide receiver, digs hard across the middle as Bert drops back. McDougall is about ten yards out when he holds up his hands. Bert lets it go. But just as the ball spirals off the tips of Bert's fingers, McDougall plants his foot and cuts for the corner of the end zone.

Bert watches the ball bounce a yard or two beyond where McDougall made his cut. McDougall is also watching the ball. Everybody is watching the ball bounce across the empty grass. Bert feels the weight of every eye shifting to him as he hustles out to get it.

Bert stands outside himself through the rest of the drill. He watches himself drop back, throw, move off to the side, throw again when his turn comes around. He sees with absolute clarity the difference between him and the other guys. They are at ease and he isn't. The ease—and the confidence—is in their voices, the way they take the three quick steps and plant their back foot as though there weren't a chance in the world they could stumble over their own feet, the way they throw the ball rather than aiming it as Bert does, even in the way they walk off to the side and talk with one another as though all this were fun.

Bert watches the scrimmage from the sidelines with the other guys who aren't among the first eleven on offense or defense. Before long the coaches begin substituting. To Bert's surprise, Kevin Robideaux, the fourth quarterback, goes in. They put him in before Christman, Bert thinks. They know how good Christman is, so they don't need to see him. They want to see Robideaux and me so they know who to cut. But Robideaux is a sophomore. If they've kept him on varsity through two cuts, they won't cut him now. They'll want to keep a sophomore so they'll have a guy with two years' experience by the time he's a senior. They'll cut me.

Bert has told himself he knows he won't make the team, but a part of him hasn't accepted it. A big portion of his memory and something in his body too remembers how he'd not only made every team when he was younger but been among the best players. These parts of Bert have whispered that he really is good and that the coaches will see it. But now all the various components of Bert Bowden have given in to the knowledge that he and football are parting ways for good.

Chapter 3

Bert Gives His Word Again

A quarter-mile east of the Y where Highway 2 forks off Division Street is Shepard's Classic and Custom Cycles. The old blue Sportster is still sitting in the window. A horn blares behind him as Bert spins the steering wheel and bounces his VW Bug over the curb.

Bert has only looked through the windows before, but this evening he pushes through the door and walks among the bikes.

The first three are Harleys. They look new, but as Bert reads the tags hanging from the handlebars he sees that one is a '55, one a '57, and one a '62.

Behind the Harleys sit two Nortons and two Triumphs, and in the row behind sit three BSAs. Bert has never heard of a Norton before, but he remembers seeing a BSA on a John Cougar Mellencamp CD cover. These bikes have such a simple look that they don't even seem like the same kind of vehicle as the racer-style Japanese bikes a lot of guys at school have.

The Harleys look tough in a squatty, old-timey way, and the Nortons, Triumphs, and BSAs are sleek and bright like exotic fish. All the bikes are so clean, they look like they were just made. But they were made a long time ago.

The newest is the '79 Triumph, and the oldest is the '55 Harley.

Bert doesn't know much about motorcycles, and he knows even less about music, but he believes that if rock and roll were a machine, it would be a motorcycle. These old bikes, especially the Harleys, make songs by Bob Seger and Bruce Springsteen roar in his head.

The back of the showroom opens into the shop, and this is where Bert sees Shepard. The man stands beside a rusty old wreck of a motorcycle strapped to a workstand, scrutinizing the nasty thing and making notes on his clipboard. Now he turns to Bert.

"Wheat farmer from down around Reardon brought an old Triumph in last winter," Shepard says. He gestures at the bike with his clipboard. "It was in worse shape than this. Guy said it'd been leaning against his windmill since 1959.

"I got it up on the stand and was looking it over," he says. "I stuck my face down where the dynamo should have been and shined my penlight in the mounting hole. Two little black eyes shined right back at me, and I thought I saw a forked tongue whipping."

Shepard turns and sets the clipboard on the bench. "I let out a scream and went up in the air," he says. "I came down about halfway across the room." He pulls a long metal bar from a set of bars in graduated sizes hanging on the pegboard above the bench and holds it up. "I grabbed this breaker bar, and I went back and tapped on the dynamo housing. No response from the snake. So I poked around in there and fished him out." He returns the bar to its peg and walks toward Bert.

"You're thinking that snake was dead, right?" Shepard says.

Bert isn't terribly comfortable here in a place he's never been before with this big man walking toward him. He smiles a nervous smile and shrugs.

"He looked dead," Shepard says. "He felt dead. He didn't smell dead, though, which should have told me something. I tossed him in the trash barrel back by the wood stove." He points his thumb toward the back of the shop.

"About a half hour later I'm dumping a worthless fairing in the trash and that snake goes off like a school bell. He'd been hibernating in that dynamo housing," Shepard says. "Thing had nine rattles." He smiles now, and there's a quality in his face that puts Bert at ease.

"So, son," Shepard says—and he's right in front of Bert now, so tall, Bert has to lift his head to look him in the face—"don't ever let anyone tell you restoring motorcycles is for sissies."

"Nobody could convince me of it" is Bert's reply.

Shepard laughs. "Well, that's good," he says.

Shepard walks along the line of classic bikes and Bert walks beside him. He tells Bert he remembers him, that Bert is the cause of the shop going over their yearly budget for Glass Plus because Bert drooled so heavily on the window where the Sportster sits. Bert smiles and says he stopped to look at it once or twice. In front of the old Sportster is where they stop now.

The bike looks bigger today. It's more sharply defined against the air and the objects around it. Everything evaporates from Bert's thoughts but the image of this machine and his related imaginings. Nothing hurts now. He wonders if he could be a different guy on this motorcycle.

"I've dropped the price to eleven hundred," Shepard says. "My boy's come to stay with me, and we want to put a hot tub in. We've got everything ready except the tub itself, and I can't find anybody who'll trade for one or let me work for it. So I need eleven hundred dollars cash money."

God, Bert thinks, eleven hundred bucks! I can buy it! He looks past the motorcycle to the window where it and he and Shepard are reflected. He would pay every cent of his savings to feel the way he looks in this reflection.

"I don't know much about motorcycles," Bert says. "I just think it's a beautiful thing." God, Bert asks himself, why did I say that?

"I do too," Shepard says. He sweeps his hand from the Sportster to the other bikes. "I think they're all beautiful things.

"What a guy's got to consider," Shepard goes on, "is that these older Harleys—all the classic bikes, for that matter—aren't like Japanese bikes. They require maintenance. If a guy just wants to ride, he should have a Japanese bike. Get a good used Honda for five hundred bucks, change the oil once a year, adjust the valves every decade, and you'll be riding it the rest of your life."

He steps up to the Sportster. "The old bikes don't go as fast or stop as fast," he says. He points to the front wheel. "No disk brakes." He points to the forks. "Inferior suspension." He raps the gas tank. "Worse fuel economy." He moves his fingers over the leather seat. "Not as comfortable." He points with his left hand to the little headlight and to the taillight with his right. "Inferior lighting. These weren't made to run the lights all the time, which is the law now. And you can't just push a button to start 'em."

The glow begins to fade from Bert's face.

Shepard walks past the bike to the corner of the room, grabs an aluminum loading ramp and returns. "You do, however, get the pleasure and the challenge of kick-starting these."

He places one end of the ramp on the edge of the platform where the bike sits and the other end on the floor, then he steps up onto the platform. "And there's no sound I know of in the world of machines that's as sweet as the exhaust note of a Harley-Davidson V-twin," he says.

Shepard rolls the Sportster forward, then lifts the back wheel and sets it square with the ramp. "What's your name?" he asks.

"Bert Bowden," Bert says.

"Well, Bert, I'll let this thing down as easy as I can,

and you keep it from rolling across the floor and busting up the place," Shepard says. "I'm Scotty."

Bert holds the rear fender brace and steps backward, pushing against the rolling weight. In a second the bike is flat on the floor. He holds the door as Shepard pushes the Sportster out onto the asphalt. The big man has a limp, and Bert wonders if he got it falling off a motorcycle. Bert watches him more closely and sees that both his legs are bad. Shepard lets the bike settle onto its sidestand. "Throw a leg over," he says.

Bert climbs on, tips the bike off the stand, and keeps it steady with his legs. It's heavy, and it sits high. But it's really neat. It's like a chunk of condensed power there beneath him.

"Can you still get parts for these?" Bert asks. He knows his dad would ask that. He wishes he hadn't thought of his dad. His dad hates motorcycles even more than his mom does. Bert's father is an insurance man.

"No problem on spares," Shepard replies. "What you can't get as original equipment is being remanufactured." He takes a step closer. "Now you're going to light this thing up," he says.

Light it up? Bert thinks.

They turn on the fuel tap and retard the spark by adjusting the magneto. Bert looks around for the key, but Shepard tells him there is no key. "Not many people know how to start one of these," he says. "But you're gonna know."

Shepard reaches down and pivots the kick pedal outward on the lever. He tells Bert to kick it through easy a couple times to prime the carb. Bert feels the big pistons move. They gulp air through the carburetor with a thirsty sound.

"Okay," Shepard says, "we got the gas on, spark set, carb primed, biker expression on face. Time to give 'er *a manly kick*, as the British say."

Bert rests his weight on his left leg. Then he rears up, shifts his weight to his right, and comes down hard on the pedal.

The sound of the engine is deep and mellow. Bert feels the pulse rise through him slow and measured like a heartbeat. "Okay," Shepard says, "blip the throttle."

Bert turns the throttle and the Sportster roars. The sound rises like a fist punching a hole in the world. And when Bert backs off, the exhaust makes a hard, barking sound like nasty laughter.

Shepard thumbs the red button next to the throttle and the engine dies. "That's how you shut 'er down," he says.

"I'll be here tomorrow to give you the money," Bert says. "If I had any money now, I'd give you some to hold it."

"No need," Sherpard replies. "Your word's enough."

"I give you my word, then," Bert says, and he reaches to shake Shepard's hand.

Chapter 4

Too Chickenshit to Live

Bert pulls up in front of his house, climbs out of the Bug, sets his school folder on the hood, and pulls his new Harley T-shirt over his head. Everybody who buys a bike gets a shirt, Shepard said. Bert bends down and looks at himself in the side mirror. He smooths the collar of his white Lacoste shirt over the black T-shirt. He doesn't feel like himself in tough-guy clothes. He just bought a tough-guy motorcycle, though, so some changes in his image might be due. "This could be a look for me," Bert says, thinking of Michael Keaton at the end of *Beetlejuice* when his head is shrunk.

Bert walks through the garage to the back door. He can't keep from looking down at his chest where an eagle glares out of yellow eyes and screams with its beak wide, HARLEY-DAVIDSON, TOO TOUGH TO DIE!

His dad's Acura is sitting next to his mom's Mazda. Bert was hoping his dad would be at a dinner meeting. There won't be any playing them off against each other. But the time for that is over, Bert tells himself. Time to stand up and face them both.

I'll have some shirts printed up, Bert is thinking as he lies on his bed. They'll be pink with a picture of me in a diaper, a thoughtful expression on my baby face, and above the picture they'll say ALBERT BOWDEN, and below, TOO CHICKENSHIT TO LIVE!

Bert didn't tell his parents during supper. Now *Nightline* is over and he's lying on his bed not paying attention to a *Hill Street Blues* rerun.

For a while during the evening Bert's mind was filled with images of riding the Sportster. He rode along the Spokane River through a cool green tunnel of fir trees. He rode into the school parking lot, the Sportster's exhaust note deep and mellow like a musical motif that accompanies the hero in a movie.

But Bert wants a real image of himself he can admire for a change instead of a fantasy, and it is in pursuit of this that he arises from his bed, walks upstairs, and knocks on his parents' bedroom door.

"Bert?" his mother says.

"Yeah," Bert says. "I need to talk to you guys."

"Well, come in," she says.

Bert sits at the foot of his mother's bed. Her reading lamp is on, but it only illuminates a circle the size of a basketball on her pillow. Bert's father is just a dark shape turning and sitting up against the headboard of his bed a few feet away. "Jesus, Bert," comes the voice from the dark shape. "We've got to work tomorrow."

"I bought that Harley-Davidson motorcycle I told you guys about," Bert says.

The dark shape sits straighter. His mother doesn't

move. "What can we do, Donald?" she finally says.

"You can't do anything," Bert says. "You don't need to do anything."

"Of course we can do something," Donald Bowden says. "You're sixteen years old. You can't enter into a contract without our permission."

"Jesus, Dad," Bert says. "That's not the point." Bert shakes his head. He can see the mixture of disapproval and scorn on his mom's face, but his dad is just a voice and a shape in the dark.

"It doesn't matter how much it cost, Bert," his mother says. "That money is for college."

"College is two years away, Mom. If I can get in at all. I don't need money for college right now. I need this motorcycle."

"Human beings need food, water, protection from the cold," his father says. "We might have a physical need for affection. But nobody needs a goddamn motorcycle."

That's right, Bert says to himself. What kind of a human being thinks he needs a motorcycle?

"Where's the bike?" his father asks.

"It's still at the shop."

"Good," his father says. "Then you won't have to take it back."

"Dad, I gave my word."

"You can take your word back. Taking your word back isn't lying," Bert's father says. "If you're concerned about integrity, you might give some thought to the fact that we said you couldn't buy that motorcycle, and you said okay. And you might consider that you live in our house, and that as a matter of integrity you might abide by our rules.

"We've told you, and told you, and told you, Bert," his father goes on. "It wouldn't matter if you had a million dollars in the bank and a full ride to Stanford, we wouldn't let you buy a motorcycle because they're too dangerous. Motorcycles kill and maim thousands of people every year. It's the ones who survive and lie in hospital beds like veg—"

Bert is up and screaming into the dark. "I don't need a motorcycle wreck to turn me into a vegetable. I'm a vegetable now! I'm a fucking vegetable right now!"

Bert is out the door, down the hall, and halfway across the kitchen. He takes a half-dozen deep breaths as he stands at the sink looking out the window into the dark. He listens for his father's footsteps. He drinks a glass of water. He's sure his mother will come out. He drinks another glass of water. The house is silent except for water dripping into the drain. Neither his mother nor his father comes after him. Bert can't think of a thing to do but go back to his room.

Bert walks around three sides of his bed and back, around and back. He hates it that he's not going to buy the Sportster. He hates it that he's going to break his word. And he hates it most that he doesn't have the guts to do what he wants to do.

Maybe this is the worst thing that ever happened to him. He needs to start writing that essay. But he needs to apologize to his folks first.

A milestone, Bert thinks as he walks upstairs, I said "fuck" in front of my mom and dad.

Bert hears voices behind the door, so he hesitates before knocking. He puts his hear to the door to hear his father's words.

"Bert was such a bright kid when he was younger," Donald Bowden is saying. "I don't know what happened. It seems like he gets dimmer every year. I don't know if there's anything in there anymore. He's just become this zero. A nothing."

Bert turns and walks quietly down the hall, through the kitchen and downstairs. He pulls his green-and-gold Thompson High athletic bag from his closet shelf and tosses it on his bed. He takes his savings book from the drawer of his nightstand, removes the seventy-one dollars from between the pages, puts the cash in his wallet, then throws the wallet and savings book in the bag. He tosses in some clothes, then walks to the bathroom and grabs his toothbrush and toothpaste. He steps into his Reeboks, pulls on the Harley T-shirt, and looks around the room. He sees his school folder on the desk and grabs it along with two pens. This is all he needs for tonight. He can come back tomorrow before his folks get home from work. He turns off the light and heads upstairs once more.

Bert leaves a note on the fridge telling his parents not to worry, that he's spending the night in a motel, then he'll find a room to rent. He tells them they're right, he should abide by their rules if he's going to live in their house. But this is a rule he can't abide, so he's moving out. He says he'll be careful on his motorcycle.

Chapter 5

Everything Changes

Bert feels an unexpected sense of adventure as he pushes the Bug to the end of the block. He's pushed the sixteen-year-old car plenty of times, but it's never pushed this easily. Bert is energized. He feels like he could stay up all night, and he's going to have to if he wants to finish his English essay. Which he will do.

Bert gives a final push and lets the Bug roll through the intersection and down the gentle slope of the Susan B. Anthony Elementary School parking lot. He follows, looking up at the stars.

God, what a beautiful night. The air is cool, like water on his face and neck and arms. Bert is scared, but that's okay. He should be a little scared if he's going to face this.

He walks through the lot and across the grass and sits on one of the swings. These are the swings he swung on all through his childhood. This is where he started school. He remembers his first day of kindergarten like it was yesterday. He can hear the teacher call out the names: Steven Thonski, Janice Fluman, Jeannie Knutsen, Kyle Retger, Pat Sweat. He can see their faces. He was scared of all the boys.

"Everything changes," Bert says aloud in the dark. The creaking of the chains and the wind whistling softly in his ears as he pumps high are the only sounds.

Everything changes, he says to himself again. And I can change too. If I changed once for the worse, I can change again for the better. I can be somebody different from who I am now.

Bert thinks of the days when he fit comfortably on the seat of this little-kids' swing. He loved school then. There were always other kids to play with, always something new to learn, assignments he could take home and do with ease and find a star or a bird sticker on when the teacher returned them. It seemed like Bert knew the answer to every question the teachers asked then. He thought he knew all the answers, anyway, and he sure tried to answer all the questions. Until fifth grade, that is. That's when things began to go bad.

And now, at one o'clock in the morning as he swings on the little-kids' swings, Bert realizes the worst thing that ever happened to him. He digs his heels into the dirt to stop himself. He walks fast across the playground, climbs into the Bug, fires it up, and heads to town to find a motel. He's got an essay to write.

Chapter 6

Bert Keeps His Word

The motel clock-radio erupts in Rolling Stones at the same time the wake-up call buzzes. The exact same time, Bert thinks. It's amazing! It's a sign!

The Stones are suffering mixed emotions at high volume. Bert Bowden, however, is possessed of singular conviction as he sits on the edge of the bed and speaks aloud. "I consider this roughly akin to the Holy Virgin appearing in cloud formations over the state of Wisconsin. What we have here, ladies and gentlemen, is a miracle. This," he says as he shuffles toward the shower like Beetlejuice heading for the whorehouse, "is the way to begin a day."

When Bert reaches the bathroom door, he turns and faces the room, bends his knees, thrusts out his crotch, and grabs himself in what strikes him as an appropriate gesture of masculine affirmation. "Honk! Honk!" he says to the empty room, to the day, to this new life he is beginning.

Bert's high spirits evaporate at roughly the same time his cup of complimentary motel coffee is empty. Bert is not used to drinking coffee. As he waits at the light watching the kids in the mall parking lot sitting on the fenders of their cars talking, laughing, listening to music, he is sure he feels the corrosive liquid working its way through his stomach. Not the way stuff is supposed to go through a stomach, but eating through the lining, bubbling back out the top, spilling like toxic waste through a flawed container.

And Bert is indeed a flawed container this morning. He's not used to drinking coffee and he's not used to functioning on three hours' sleep. The light goes green and the motorheads behind him are on their horns in a millisecond. Bert's stomach makes sounds like a volcanic mud pot as he accelerates through the light. By the time he has covered the last mile, ridden the roller coaster of speed bumps into the school lot, and slipped the Bug between two yellow lines, a band of pain has emerged inside his head and is trying to expand its way through his skull at the equator of his eyes.

Bert breathes through his mouth as he walks by the office. There's a good chance he'll throw up. The fulmination in his stomach is producing gas bubbles the size of carp. Some rise to the surface, and others dive to the depths. Maybe if he allows a little one—just a little minnow-sized one—out the lower pipe, he'll feel better. He's passing the trophy cases, his head bent, his eyes open just enough so he can see a few inches beyond the toes of his Reeboks, when he lets one go.

Most of Bert's sensory awareness is concentrated in his head where the pain is, but there's enough feeling left below to alert him to emergency conditions there as well. That is not gas escaping down here, the nerve fibers on the backs of Bert's legs tell him. If this were once vapor, it has now condensed into something more substantial.

You have shit yourself, Dude. And in the main hall at school. How's that for the way to begin a day? How's that for a new life?

Bert stops to lean his forehead against the cool glass of the trophy case and sees that he has come undone in the most ironic of locations: in front of the epitome of self-discipline, the late Louden Swain, Thompson High's Olympic wrestler, Spokane's famous astronaut.

Bert steps back and looks into the photo. The crew, in full gear, stands in front of the space shuttle. Swain is smiling like a little kid, like he can't wait to get up there on top of that rocket and have somebody light the fuse. Bert reads, as he has read many times, the lines in memoriam:

> **Major Louden Swain, USAF, Thompson**
> **High Class of 1972. Born December 2, 1954,**
> **Spokane, Washington; died January 22, 1985,**
> **on his way to space.**

Usually Bert reads in these lines the message that heroism is possible. But this morning the message is this: Some people are something and some people are nothing. And you, Bert Bowden, are among the nothings.

At least I can keep my word, Bert thinks on his way to the bathroom. I can do that, at least. He continues to tell himself this on his way to Tanneran's room.

But Tanneran isn't there, and he isn't in the journalism room next door. A girl looks up from a keyboard and says The Big T is in the darkroom.

Bert can't wait long. He'll have to disturb him. He crosses the room and knocks. A voice that's not Tanneran's yells, "Don't open that door!"

"I'm sorry to bother you," Bert says. "My name is Bert Bowden, and I need to see Mr. Tanneran."

Half a minute later the door opens. At first it's like a cave—deep black, just tinged with a purple glow at the end. But then it floods with light. A guy with fuzzy red hair like Poindexter, the guy with thick glasses in *Revenge of the Nerds*, stands at the back of the room holding a pair of long tweezers in front of his chest like a sword and glaring. Another guy, an Asian, is hanging photos on a wire. Tanneran is standing beside this shorter kid looking at the photos, then turns and walks toward Bert. "Close the door, please," says the redheaded kid. And Tanneran closes the door.

"Bert Bowden," Tanneran says. He looks at the sheet of paper Bert holds out to him. "The young man who keeps his word."

"I'm sorry to bother you," Bert says. "But I'm not feeling well, and I want to give you the essay before I go home."

Tanneran takes the sheets. "One, two, three . . . fourteen pages," he counts. "Good Lord!"

"I would have typed it, but I wasn't where my computer was," Bert says.

"Go home and go to bed," Tanneran says. "You look bad."

"I feel bad," Bert says.

On his way to the car Bert sees a crowd of football players at the gym door. They are jocking around like yearling killer whales when it's raining fish. The cut-list has been posted. Mike Jackson and Christman and McDougall and other guys who didn't have a worry in the world about getting cut are high- and low-fiving Camille Shepard.

Bert squeezes through. He reads the names. He reads down the list again. It's no surprise that his name is not here. It's no surprise, but it hurts.

He will walk to his car. He will drive to the bank. He will buy the Sportster. He will keep his word.

Chapter 7

Scott Shepard Meets Bert's Father and Resolves to Return a Kindness

Donald Bowden observed the woman and the two bikers from the McDonald's lot across the highway. She sat in a green sports car with the top down. She was in her mid-thirties, wore her straw-blond hair in a long, thick braid, and radiated that healthier-than-thou attitude Donald found so detestably attractive.

The older guy sat on his bike with his arms folded, smiling. There was gray in his hair, the stubble of his beard, and his moustache. The younger guy wore an old-fashioned black half-helmet out of which his ponytail hung. They were both big.

Donald would not have been surprised to see the three exchange drugs, but they exchanged only smiles, and then waves as the woman sped away.

The younger biker dismounted, walked to the older biker, and kissed him on the cheek. Donald watched them knock their fists together like steroid-addled athletes, vicious subliterate pimps, dumbass bikers. Then the younger one returned to his bike, kicked it into a roar, and shot out through the colored band of cars like a black bullet through a rainbow.

The older guy left his bike and walked to the door of the shop. This must be Shepard, Donald said to himself.

Scott Shepard watched his son sitting at the light, revving his engine. Aside from his worry about Camille's safety on the Harley-Davidson, Shepard felt a profound sense of peace. It was a sense that his life had finally dialed itself in and was running right.

Camille chirped the tire when the light went green. His father's heart did a wheelstand. "Stay off your head!" the elder Shepard yelled. But the younger was long gone.

Shepard walked up to open the door. He was standing in the doorway looking out at the beautiful early September morning when the silver Acura pulled up. A man in a suit stepped out. His jaw was set as he started for the door. Shepard couldn't remember having done anything that would occasion such an aggressive posture in someone this well dressed.

"My name is Donald Bowden," Donald said. He wondered if the guy would want to do some stupid power handshake.

Shepard shook Donald's hand in the traditional way. "I'm Scott Shepard," he said. "People call me Scotty. I'll bet you're Bert Bowden's dad."

"I'm Bert's father, and I'm upset," Donald replied.

The kid must take after his mother, Shepard thought. This guy is dark, wiry, over six feet. "Step inside, Mr. Bowden," he said. "Let's get you pacified."

Donald looked up at Shepard. The man filled the

doorway in height and width. Donald was six two, and not accustomed to looking up at people. He wasn't intimidated by Shepard, but he was surprised the man spoke standard English. He followed him across the showroom to the counter. Shepard hung his jacket on a peg and turned. "Your son doesn't want the bike? You don't want him to have the bike? What?" he said.

Donald was looking at the tattooed letters on Shepard's forearm. RIDE FAST, LIVE FOREVER, they said. He's a moron, all right, Donald thought. His philosophy of life is not only self-contradictory, it's brief enough to wear on his arm.

"He wants the bike," Donald replied. "He wants it bad enough to have moved out of the house when his mother and I told him he wasn't buying it. We don't even know where he slept last night."

"Maybe he's embarrassed," Shepard said. "I won't give him a hard time. I've got a teenage boy of my own."

"We've decided to let him buy the motorcycle," Donald said. "He's never acted like this before, so he must need to have it worse than we need him not to." Donald looked steadily into Shepard's face. "It was a shitty thing to take advantage of a kid like Bert," he said.

Kid like Bert? Shepard thought. He thought a second or two more. "Maybe I did take advantage of his enthusiasm," he replied. "I tried to get him to consider the downside of owning a classic bike, but maybe I didn't try hard enough. I'm sorry I had a part in bringing trouble into your home," he said.

Donald felt better. He'd said his piece, taken care of business, and now he was ready to get out of this place.

Shepard followed him to the door. "When Bert shows up I'll tell him he's out of the doghouse."

Donald Bowden climbed into his car and drove off without a reply.

Shepard got the coffee going and turned on *All Things Considered*. His partner would come rolling in soon. They would drink coffee, do some light work, and yell at the radio until the news was over.

National Public Radio was interviewing members of Congress about President Bush's battle plan for his war on drugs. Another morning this would have held Shepard's attention. Nine years ago Shepard was pensioned out of the Bureau of Alcohol, Tobacco and Firearms, and news of this kind involved men and women who were still his friends. But this morning his thoughts were on two boys—his own and Donald Bowden's.

Shepard stepped to his tool chest and lifted the top. Taped to the inside were photos of Camille from age two, when his mother took him to live in Paris, to eight, which was the last time he came to the States for a visit. Shepard had flown to Paris for Camille's thirteenth birthday, and then they hadn't seen each other until three months ago when Camille came to spend his senior year of high school.

None of the photos looked much like the boy who had ridden off on his motorcycle a few minutes before. He'd shed his baby fat, grown six inches in four years, and his hair had darkened. It was no point of pride with Shepard, but now Camille looked more like a Shepard than a Laval.

More important than how the kid looked was how he felt, and as far as Shepard could see he was a happy boy. He kept looking for cracks in his son's character that would signal the fault he was afraid had to be there somewhere as a result of this transcontinental family life. But he hadn't spotted any yet. It could be, he supposed, that the son had not been critically flawed by the father. If this were so, it was a stroke of good luck Shepard knew he didn't deserve. Camille deserved it, of course. All kids deserved good luck.

Scott Shepard didn't believe in a loving God, nor did he believe in a just universe. He did not believe that in life or afterward people got what they deserved. If people sometimes seemed to get what was coming to them, Shepard figured it was a fortunate accident. He did, however, try to live his life as though justice would be dealt out to him sometime, somehow. He wished life were this way, he thought it should be this way, so this was how he tried to live it.

Shepard turned away from the photos, but he could still see them in his mind. They were always there.

So many people on both sides of the Atlantic had been kind to his son. If this were not so, Camille would not be the happy kid he was. His mother, his stepfather, his grandparents, teachers, coaches, his day-care mom and their families, his therapist when he was six. Shepard knew some of these people well, some he'd met, some he was able to imagine from what Camille told him, and others had shown his son kindness, love, patience, had treated the boy decently, and would never pass through Shepard's thoughts where he could thank them face to imagined face.

There was luck in the way his boy had turned out, of course. But there were also these good people. Some of them got paid to be good to kids, but that didn't matter. Plenty of people got paid to be good to kids and treated them like shit.

Whatever opportunity Shepard had to be kind to Bert Bowden, he would take. Maybe Bert was Shepard's chance to return some water to the well.

Chapter 8

Bert Keeps His Word Again

Bert withdrew fifteen hundred bucks from savings for the bike and a jacket. His parents haven't alerted the bank as he feared. The fifteen one-hundred-dollar bills lie in a bank envelope on the passenger seat of the Bug, which Bert pilots north on Division. He can stay on this road, cross the Little Spokane River, climb the hill on the other side of the valley, and keep going until he burrows into the mountains. But he won't burrow into the mountains today. Today Bert will keep is word.

Shepard is sitting in the back of the shop playing cribbage on an empty shopstand with his partner, Dave Ward, who looks like Billy Gibbons, guitarist for ZZ Top. Dave's gray beard reaches to the cribbage board and enmeshes like cobwebs the green and red plastic pegs. They didn't hear Bert come in, and they don't notice him standing beside the cash register. He clears his throat, and both men turn.

"Bert Bowden," Shepard says. "Had lunch?" He gestures with a remnant of fishwich. "I could eat a couple more of these."

Bert is feeling better. He could eat something. But "I

came to pay for the Sportster" is what he replies.

"Let's pop across the road, get a bite, and talk about that," Shepard says.

Bert and Shepard are standing on the island waiting for a break in traffic when Bert realizes they are wearing identical T-shirts as well as jeans in the same degree of fade. The faces in the car windows all turn with looks of disapproval. Biker and biker junior, the looks say.

Shepard can really motor for a guy with two bad legs. Bert is hustling after him, taking note of this, as the toe of his Reebok catches the curb. He is airborne. He throws his hands out and knows that for him today's lunch will be fillet of concrete. But Shepard catches him at the shoulder.

Bert gains altitude as he flies over the sidewalk. Shepard is lifting him. Bert feels his weight shifting in relation to the fulcrum that Shepard is making of his shoulder joint. This guy is holding me in the air with one arm, Bert thinks as he descends against the tension Shepard applies.

Bert hears a crack simultaneous with his landing. That sounds an awful lot like bone, he thinks. But I'm not in pain. He looks down. He has landed in a low shrub. Each of his tennies rests on a branch, and at the base of each branch the wet white flesh of the shrub is open in a compound fracture.

"Oops," comes Shepard's voice from behind him.

Shepard eats a fishwich while he tells Bert that his dad

visited the shop and he no longer needs to look for new lodgings. Bert works on a fourteen-box of McNuggets and listens. This is good news. He's already begun to miss his room.

Shepard gives Bert a chance to back out of the deal. He notes again the various ways classic bikes can be a pain in the ass. He reminds Bert that this is the month of September, and that if they're lucky with the weather and wear their longies, they have until Thanksgiving before they put the bikes away. Shepard can't guarantee that the Sportster won't sell, but he can guarantee he'll have something really neat for Bert to buy for the same money come spring. He can understand that Bert wants to keep his word. But coming back when he said he would is more integrity than most people show.

No, Bert wants the bike.

Is Bert aware that he needs a motorcycle endorsement for his driver's license? Yes, Bert knows that. Has he heard how nasty the test is? Not exactly. But how tough can it be? Other people pass it. True, Shepard agrees. Not only true, but an excellent way to look at it.

"I guess I can't talk you out of this," Shepard says.

"If you don't want to sell it—"

"No," Shepard says. "I'm happy to sell it. You're acting out of integrity, and I'm trying to act out of integrity too. I don't want you to feel stuck."

"I don't feel stuck," Bert says.

"Okay," Shepard replies. "But let's say this: You decide

you want to sell the bike, you bring it back and we'll get you at least what you paid for it, plus the tax and license."

"Okay," Bert says.

"Let's go do the deed, then."

"Let's go do it," Bert says.

And they go and do it.

Chapter 9

Reflection

Bert looks down at his motorcycle. He owns a 1969 Harley-Davidson Sportster. He can't believe it. He twists the throttle and the tension running from his hand into his forearm is a thrill. He really cannot believe it. And yet these are real, physical sensations: the hard rubber handle grip tight against his palm, the cold cement floor of the garage against the bare soles of his feet. It's not a dream. It's like a dream, but it's not one.

Bert Bowden owns this old motorcycle, all right. And he's also got a permit to ride it—during the day in the company of a licensed rider. After Bert signed the papers at Shepard's, he drove to the license bureau, read the booklet, took the written test, and only missed one question. When he feels confident enough on the bike, he'll take the riding test. He drove back to Shepard's, then rode the Sportster home and tucked it away in the garage. It was scary, but Shepard rode beside him and they took the less traveled roads. Bert sat behind Shepard on the way back to the shop to get the Bug. Bert didn't know where to put his hands at first, and Shepard told him just to set them on his shoulders. The little pillion seat on the rear fender made Bert sit higher than Shepard, and it felt natural to rest his hands on the man's shoulders.

Bert knows only one thing that feels as neat as riding a Harley-Davidson motorcycle.

For the zillionth time tonight Bert mounts the bike. The leather seat is hard against his butt, smooth through the worn flannel of his pajama bottom. The steel gas tank is smooth and cold and inflexible against the insides of his knees. This is not a dream. And yet, as in a dream, there's a quality here that says this is some other kind of reality.

Bert grips the bars with both hands, tips the bike up off the side stand, and holds it straight and steady with the strength of his legs. He tenses his body against the shock of acceleration and takes off, vibrating his lips in a motor sound. But the sound of vibrating lips is so unlike the roar of a Harley-Davidson V-twin, and Bert makes such an unlikely biker in his jammies and bare feet here in the garage in the narrow space between the wall and his parents' cars, that even though no ears hear him but his own and no other eyes see, he is embarrassed.

Bert leans the bike back down on its stand and dismounts. He can't stop looking at it. It will take some getting used to, like Shepard said. But Bert will have patience and he will get used to the Sportster. He looks down at his face reflected in the round chrome air-cleaner. That is his face shining there with the words "Harley-Davidson Motor Co." embossed upon it. The image is distorted, but that is Bert Bowden's face.

Chapter 10

Bowdenland

Bert is so tired. He told himself he'd earned a good sleep. He'd turned in his essay and he bought the bike. He couldn't buy a jacket because Scotty doesn't sell them; he'll order one from L.L. Bean. He'd passed the written test for his learner's permit. He can ride during the day in the company of a licensed rider. When he passes the riding exam, he'll receive his operator's license and be on his own.

Bert is beat and he deserves a rest. But here he lies with his eyes cranked open. There's a lot to see in the darkness bristling above his bed, and he sees it even more clearly when he closes his eyes.

He sees himself eight hours earlier riding the Sportster alongside Scott Shepard. They ride through a roaring tunnel. Bert feels the wind, the tiny particles of sand that swirl against his cheeks and around his glasses into his eyes. He feels these things and he sees the soft-blue fall sky, the foothills to the east, blue-black where the pine trees grow, yellow where the farmers have cut and baled the year's last hay, and brown where they've already turned the ground.

Bert didn't do a bad job on his first ride. He got the Sportster started on the third kick, he shifted smoothly up and down through the gears. He stalled when he tried to get going again at a stop sign, but he fired it back up and ran the speedo needle almost to fifty as he sped to catch Shepard.

Bert sees the red tip of the speedo needle move up and down the circle of numbers as he lies in bed with his eyes closed. He feels the throttle in his hand. His hand makes the needle move. His hand turns the growl of the engine into a roar and the roar into a tunnel of sound that shuts out the world. In this direction lies Bowdenland, where for a few seconds Bert makes a world of his own.

Outside the transparent walls of the tunnel Bert sees the people who have come to watch him on his journey tonight. Tonight they stand along the road Bert rides on his new old motorcycle. On other nights the way to Bowdenland leads through the football field, and the people stand on the sidelines watching; or down the main hall at school where they sit on the benches and watch as Bert walks by; or in the mall where they line the rail on the second floor and look down at Bert looking into the windows of the Benetton store where the clothes hang perfectly on the mannequins and where the models in the floor-to-ceiling murals don't care that they're geeks; or in the mountains where they stand in the meadow like deer and watch Bert sitting by a stream, a handline held between his thumb and index finger.

Always watched and always watching. But it's the only way to get to Bowdenland.

When Bert dips into his thoughts for a girl or woman to accompany him, every single thing in that sixteen-year-old bag of his brain comes tumbling out with her. Good things and bad things and things that don't even seem to belong to Bert spill out. And the whole mess lines up along the road to Bowdenland and watches. Bert can shut it out, but he can't make it go away. Except in those few seconds when he gets there and he's the one who makes the world.

Tonight Bert shuts it out with the sustained exhaust note of a Harley-Davidson Sportster.

His grandfather is there. He's the man he used to be. He smiles. His lips move. Bert knows the words: *Berty Boy*.

His parents stand at the side of the road. They look in his direction, but their faces are expressionless, as though there's nothing to see. At dinner they didn't say a word about where Bert slept last night. In the middle of *WKRP*, Bert's dad told him he'd have to pay his own liability insurance. Then he fell asleep on the couch. Bert watches his parents' faces as they turn and walk in different directions.

Tanneran is there, looking out over his lectern. Scott Shepard is there. He's leaning up against the chain-link fence that surrounds the practice field. The scary biker stands beside him.

Mr. Lawler, Bert's fifth- and sixth-grade teacher, is there. He stands in front of the class instructing the kids to point at Bert when he speaks without being called on. No talking, Lawler tells the class, no disruption, just thirty pointed fingers to remind young Mr. Bowden to raise his hand and wait to be called on. The kids turn and point their fingers.

Bert sees himself at the age of eleven looking back at the elevated arms and pointed fingers of his classmates. I'd forget, Bert thinks. I'd get excited because I knew the answer, and I'd just forget.

Five years go by in a single beat of Bert's heart. The metalheads are there, lounging on the hill at the edge of the school parking lot. Rick Curtis, Captain Metalhead, commands their attention along with Rick's girl Sheena. Rick plays his guitar, and Sheena plays Rick's thigh. Sheena is so alluring in her lanky, dusky, long-grackley-haired way that Bert forgives her stupid name. She is a stunning, crippling, leather-bound, smoke-sodden accident that Bert wishes would happen to him. She is every gaping light socket into which Bert ever desired to place his tongue. She is the long, black bundle of microwaves that will roast Bert in his water bed without melting the plastic.

Bert cranks the throttle and the roar of his engine nears its peak. He's revving right up to the red line. And Sheena hears it. And she turns. And she looks. And she unwinds like tentacles her long arms and legs from Rick. And she gets up and walks through the side of the tunnel into the roar.

Bert eases back on the throttle. He slows for Sheena. He will take her on a trip for which he needs no permit, no license, no indulgence of any sort except the indulgence of his own will. It is in the exercise of this will that Bert creates Bowdenland.

But the girl who climbs on isn't Sheena. It's the girl from the journalism room.

Bert doesn't know her name. He has only seen her one time. But he likes her looks. Her face is kind, intelligent. The potential for mischief shines in her eyes. This girl is nothing like Sheena, Sheena, the Metal Queena. And Bert likes her looks.

Together they ride to the top of the hill. Bert does not slow by a single rpm as they crest the summit and keep on going, airborne, into the roaring heart of Bowdenland.

Then they fall slowly, gently. Yes, they fall sweetly. It is not a far fall any night, and tonight it is particularly short, although no less sweet. As always, Bert hits the ground alone. Alone and unobserving he crosses the border into unobserved sleep.

Chapter 11

Young Mr. Bowden

Bert Bowden

Junior English

September 6, 1989

THE WORST THING THAT EVER HAPPENED TO ME

Most of the fourth-grade boys faked anxiety when Ms. Pinkus, our principal, informed us on the last day of school that a man would be teaching fifth grade in the fall. He would be our first male teacher.

Ms. Pinkus did not imply that this man would be more strict than the women, but some of the boys reacted as though this would be so. I myself tumbled onto the floor and convulsed in an imitation of cattle-prod torture. That's the kind of kid I was.

On our way home my friends and I were giddy with visions of our summer vacation and also with the prospect of a dramatic turn in our lives: a man teacher. We would have to toe the line. But it would be good for us. We pretended to dread that first day of school in the fall when we would find out who got the man. I think we were all hoping to get him though. I was hoping to.

But it was already a done thing. Ms. Pinkus and Ms. Waters, my teacher, had talked it over with my folks, and they agreed that a male figure might have a settling influence on me in the class-room. So I got what I was hoping for. I got the man.

His name was Gary Lawler. He was a first-year teacher in his early twenties, a good-looking guy with the dark, chiseled face people think of as classically handsome. He was a little guy, maybe five six. I was big for my age, and I didn't have to look up much to meet him eye to eye. He was wiry and a fast runner, but surprisingly uncoordinated and slow to react. I wasn't as fast, but I was quick and well coordinated. I could always nail him in dodgeball, but he had to run me down before he could hit me. He'd hold the ball out and just touch me with it, or bounce it off my forehead as I stood there like a captured felon.

When recess was over he would throw his arms around the shoulders of a couple of kids and start singing. It would be a song from an old TV show like The Beverly Hillbillies *or* Mister Ed. *Other kids would link arms, then more kids would join up until there would be this long line of singing, skipping kids headed back into the building.*

He knew the words to all these TV theme songs, and pretty soon we did too. Not everybody joined in at first, but it didn't take a week before all of us—except Jim Zimster, who wouldn't do anything with anybody—were linked up. The first day of school Lawler tried pushing Zimster's wheelchair, but Zimster clamped on the brakes and wouldn't let go, and Lawler never tried it again.

Lawler put the same energy into the classroom that he put into recess. He'd divide us into teams and send one kid from each team to the board. We'd cheer if our teammate spelled the word right or worked the problem correctly fastest or named the right state capital, and we'd boo if the other team beat us to it. Lawler cheered the right answers and booed the wrong ones along with us in a good-natured way.

We weren't supposed to make too much noise or we'd disturb the other classes. But I was having so much fun I couldn't control myself. I'd get too loud, jump out of my chair, shout the answer when it wasn't my turn. All the questions were so easy. I'd groan when our kid didn't get it. I wasn't really mad, and I didn't want to hurt feelings, although I'm sure I hurt some.

Lawler would banish me to a back corner of the room for speaking out of turn. It was a small price to pay for having fun, plus, I thrived on the attention. I'd carry my desk-chair back into the sunny corner where the plants were, then I'd go get the big dictionary from his desk and start copying it, which was a punishment I enjoyed and am thankful for to this day.

I worked hard for Mr. Lawler's recognition. I tried to do what he told me. I tried to remember to raise my hand and wait to be called on, not to interrupt, not to run in the building, to remember that I didn't need to be first in line for everything.

We weren't even halfway through our six-game football season before Lawler, Ms. Pinkus, and my mom met to discuss my behavior.

A week after their meeting I had a meeting of my own with a therapist. His name was Dr. Crutcher. He asked me questions about myself and about school. Near the end of the hour he asked how I got the bruises around my eye and the cut on my ear. I told him I'd been running a quarterback option when somebody tripped me and I bashed my head into the ground. He smiled. I suppose he wondered if I was being abused.

Crutcher said he thought I was smart and funny, and that I could count on these qualities getting me into more trouble in the future, particularly in school. The older I got, he said, the easier it would be for me to control my behavior. He suggested that in the meantime, if I didn't want to get buried in the hole I was digging for myself at school, I'd better do what they told me.

I became a model of behavior. Things weren't as fun, but I wasn't in trouble all the time. I thought I understood how a staked dog might feel. Lawler's questions would cruise by like fat newspaper kids on cheap bicycles, and my mind would scramble off after them like a crazed Doberman. I'd get right to the edge of the grass, my sharp little fifth-grader's intellectual fangs all shiny and dripping, poised to rip jeans and sneakers, and then I'd come to the end of the rope. I'd feel it constrict around my throat, and I couldn't shout or speak in a normal tone or even whisper. I just stayed right there at the edge of the sidewalk with my paw in the air ready to be called on. But I never got called on.

I was also never one of the kids Lawler linked arms with when the bell ended recess. I am ashamed to admit this, but I wanted to be there with him at the center of that line of people singing and having fun.

I see now that this was when sports began to mean too much to me. I couldn't get the attention I needed in class, so I started going for it all in sports. In PE class and in football after school I began playing with a vengeance. It wasn't hard for me to excel because I was bigger and more coordinated than most of the other kids. But I also had this fire. If I'd been a team player it would have been a great quality. But I wasn't. I hogged the ball, yelled at kids when they dropped passes or missed tackles, and worse—like I did in class—I just ignored the kids who didn't want to play as bad as I did.

Our football team was undefeated and I was the star. I kept my stats in a ring binder with a photo of former Seahawks quarterback Jim Zorn on the cover. I was so full of myself.

One morning late in October, not many days after 220 or so American Marines were killed in Lebanon when some Shiite Muslim drove a truck full of explosives into their compound and set it off, one of the kids in class asked Lawler what the fighting was about. The bombing was all over TV and the newspapers and on the covers of magazines. It was a good question, although one probably not too many people could have answered.

Lawler said they were fighting about religion. The Jews and the Mohammedans, he said, were in league against the Christians. He said it was only one small part of an international conspiracy by the communists and other non-Christians to take over the world. Then he wrote "conspiracy" on the board and asked if any of us knew what it meant.

I knew what "conspiracy" meant, but I didn't raise my hand because I was confused by what he'd told us. It rang false after what I'd learned on the news.

I loved the news. I read my folks' Newsweek cover to cover before one of them would stomp down to my room and snatch it back, and I watched Nightline every night in bed. A lot of times something in the news would send me to my World Book encyclopedias, and I'd read about it and sometimes even read on into the related articles, which is how I learned about Islam.

What I'd learned from watching and listening and reading was that this stuff in Lebanon, like so much of the turmoil in the Third World, was a result of a colonial power—France, in this case—leaving a former colony without a sound government. The problem was that the Muslims didn't have fair representation.

Lawler was right about it being a religious war: The president of the country, who was a Christian, had been assassinated before he could take office, and then in retaliation Christian soldiers killed several hundred Palestinian civilians in a refugee camp. I knew the Jews had something to do with it because Israeli soldiers had let the Christians into the camp and watched them kill the unarmed Palestinians. I didn't know what the communists had to do with it, but everybody knew they were always up to no good.

Maybe if I hadn't had such a good football season and been so full of myself I never would have said anything, or maybe if I hadn't gotten so frustrated holding my paw in the air waiting for Lawler to toss me a question. For whatever reason, I couldn't keep my mouth shut. I knew all this stuff that I didn't think anyone else in the room or maybe the whole school knew, and I just couldn't keep it in.

"In the first place," I said, "they're not called Mohammedans. They're called Muslims, and their religion is Isla—"

That's as far as I got in my discourse. Lawler was at my seat before I could close my mouth on "Islam." In mid-stride he leaned down, grabbed each side of the writing surface of my desk-chair, and pushed it—and me—out of the row, down the aisle, and toward the back of the room.

Ours was an old school with wooden floors, and some of the boards had warped at the edges and were no longer level with the others. I felt the metal legs of the desk-chair catch on these raised boards and rip through them. The room was silent except for the squeal of the metal legs of my desk sliding over the floor and the intermittent splintering of the board edges.

My head whiplashed when the back legs of the desk cracked into the corner of the room. Lawler jerked the front of the desk around so I was flush with the side wall and facing forward. He walked to his desk then, picked up the big dictionary, walked back and dropped it onto the writing surface from a moderate height, causing it to make a moderate and almost whimsical splat. He was smiling, and he'd been smiling down into my face all through our trip across the floor.

"Mr. Bowden," Lawler said, "this corner is your home until you learn you are not the most important person in the room. I've got something to say to the class, and I want you to listen." With his middle finger he flipped open the dictionary about a quarter way. "When I finish," he said, "you are to start copying. You're familiar with the procedure."

He walked back to the front of the room. "Class," he said, "young Mr. Bowden has a problem. He thinks he's more important than the rest of us. He thinks he's got all the answers, and he thinks we can't wait to hear them. Young Mr. Bowden isn't going to grow up to have a happy life if he keeps on this way, because nobody's going to like him. He needs our help to change, and we're going to give him our help."

The plan was for my classmates to help me change by making me aware when I was acting too important. Lawler instructed everyone that in this one instance they didn't have to raise their hands and wait to be called on. If anyone saw me do something or heard me say something that suggested I thought I was more important than the rest of the class, they were to sing it right out. The class didn't take to this as fast as they took to singing with Lawler at recess, but they caught on after a while.

By Thanksgiving I quit answering questions even when I was called on. Lawler had told the class to listen for a "tone of superiority" in my voice, and a couple of kids who had never spoken up before took pleasure in this. It was a game, and everyone participated. But the novelty faded before long.

A couple of times a week Lawler pointed out my eruptions of self-importance. Since I'd quit talking in class, he noted things I did or said outside class. He described how I'd been showing off my new Eddie Bauer winter coat, for example, and asked the class if they thought it was kind of me to try to make the kids whose parents couldn't afford such a fancy coat feel envious.

I shouldn't say everyone participated. Everyone but Zimster did. This struck me as odd, because Zimster was the meanest kid I knew. And he was also smart. Sarcasm was his weapon. The only pleasure I ever saw him take in school was ridiculing other kids, reducing them—particularly pretty girls—to tears with a few slashes of his wit. He'd make fun of your looks or your clothes or stuff you said in class, and if you responded he'd just pour it on. If he ever got a peek at your mom or dad you'd hear about it the rest of the year. Nobody ever saw his folks.

I figured the opportunity to point out someone's faults would put Zimster in his glory, but he treated the whole enterprise with more than his usual contempt.

When we came back to school after Christmas vacation,

Lawler let me out of the corner. I would only speak when he asked me a question, and then I spoke every word to myself in my head before I let it out of my mouth.

A weird thing happened that spring. Lawler was the new baseball coach, and he cut me. Nearly everybody who turned out made the team, but I was among those who didn't. This isn't the weird thing I mean to speak of, but it sure rocked me. I couldn't believe it. Baseball was my sport. I played baseball better than I did anything. I was in a daze. It was like I'd separated into two kids, one of whom was always watching me and then giving me an immediate evaluation of every single thing I did, and the evaluation was always bad.

The first game was away, but the school we played was close so I rode my bike there. I'd been playing with these guys and two girls since we started T-ball, and I had to go and watch.

Our pitcher walked batter after batter. Lawler brought in the centerfielder, but he couldn't throw a strike. He tried another kid, but that kid hurt his arm. It didn't look like the top of the first would ever end. It was even embarrassing for the people watching.

This is the weird thing: Lawler walked around behind the backstop and up to where I was sitting in the bleachers. He held out the ball. "You want to pitch?" he said. I'd brought my glove with me, and I put it on and held it out. He dropped the ball in and I walked to the mound.

They bombed me. These were guys who couldn't hit me to save their mothers' lives in summer league, and they bombed me.

I was on the team after that. Lawler never said a word about it. We had a lousy season. I never played so bad.

Lawler was moving up to teach sixth grade the next year, and he told the class that any kids who wanted could be in his class the coming fall.

I was surprised to find not one single kid from our fifth-grade class in the room on the first day of sixth grade. I thought everybody loved the guy. I was there though. Lawler had told my folks it would be best for me. He said we were making progress and that one more year would have me shaped up.

I developed a stutter that fall. Lawler called on me a lot, and it was embarrassing not to be able to whip out the answer. I could live with that, but then it got so I couldn't call plays in the huddle fast enough. We'd keep getting penalized for delay-of-game. Then I couldn't call signals at the line. I'd stand over center and think the words in my mind, but I couldn't get them out of my mouth. The other me would stand across scrimmage with the defense and watch. He could call signals like Boomer Esiason—I heard him in my mind—but I couldn't get out a single sound.

The stutter went away by the time I got to high school, but by then I didn't have much to say.

I realize that what happened to me isn't a pimple on the butt of the pain a lot of kids endure by the time they're six-teen. After serious consideration, however, I believe it's the worst thing that ever happened to me.

Chapter 12

Gramp and Gran

Gramp was sitting in a plastic chair beside his bed when Bert walked into the room. Bert hadn't seen Gramp out of bed in a long time. He was held to the chair by a strap across his upper chest and a strap around each forearm. His head lolled to his shoulder. His eyes were open, but his face showed no expression. His lips quivered in a way that brought the word "palsy" to Bert's mind. For a while after they put Gramp in the home he would say to Bert, "All I can do is smoke." It wasn't long before he couldn't even smoke anymore.

Gramp had just been shaved, and a tiny pearl of shave cream clung to his earlobe. His hospital gown was bunched around his waist, and his shriveled penis made Bert think of ginger root in the vegetable bin at Rosauers. His legs were the bone-thin, reptilian legs of a turkey. A stainless steel pan sat on the floor beneath the chair.

Bert walked over and pulled the gown down around his grandfather's knees. He reached out and wiped away the shave cream with his thumb, then he stepped back. The fragrance of Aqua Velva dominated the other odors in the room, but the ineradicable stench of cigarette smoke remained.

Bert felt a hand at his elbow, and he turned as he stepped out of the doorway. "Excuse me," the aide said.

Bert didn't know her. She was taller than Bert, and hefty. She unstrapped his grandfather, lifted him with an arm around his waist, lifted the back of his gown with that hand, wiped him, then dropped the cloth onto the floor. She picked him up in both her arms like a stout bride carrying a feeble husband over the threshold and laid him gently on the bed.

"There you go, Berty Boy," she said as she held his arms up and snugged the sheet and blanket around his chest.

Bert opened his mouth to respond to his name. But the woman hadn't turned around. She was talking to Gramp, whose name was also Albert Bowden.

She turned from the bed, stepped back to the chair with the hole in its seat, bent and swept up the cloth and then the pan with the same hand. "You're the grand-son," she said as she crossed the room. She stopped in the doorway. "They told me you'd be coming by, but I haven't seen you."

Her name tag said Myrtrice Clovis. Up close Bert saw how young she was. She wasn't a woman. She was a girl not much older than he. What would it be like to work in such a place? What would it be like to have to? Bert thought. What would it be like to be named Myrtrice

Clovis? "I haven't been by as often," he said. "I've had football practice."

Why did I say that? Bert thought. I could come in the evenings, I could come on weekends. I haven't been by because I'm an ungrateful little bastard. He lowered his head, and that's when he saw the contents of the pan Myrtrice Clovis held at her hip.

"It don't seem like he knows one way or the other," she said. But Bert didn't hear this.

Three blood-black things the size of peas lay in a thin, shallow sauce of bright blood. The blood sloshed up the side of the shiny pan and the black turds rolled as she stepped out the door.

Bert shut his eyes and clenched his teeth. He clamped down with such force that his head and shoulders shook. He was trying to squash the life out of the image in his mind. He thought of the huge metal-press that finally kills the Terminator in the movie. It just keeps pressing down until the red light in his eyes goes out. Bert wanted to smash out the red light of the blood and the little black turds that shone in it like pupils in a big, three-pupiled blood-eye.

He walked over to the bed and took his grandfather's hand. It wasn't like leather. It was more like the snake skins he'd found in the woods with Gramp years ago. It was almost that translucent, almost that weightless. And it felt that dead.

Bert watched his grandfather's lips sing their silent,

palsied song. He would never hear his grandfather's
voice ring out in the world again. Bert would, however,
hear Gramp's voice in memory. It would ring out clearly
forever from that place where human beings are both
haunted and sustained.

It was after five when Bert rolled the Sportster into the
carport at his grandmother's house. The sun was low in
the west, but the light was strong and poured through the
blue corrugated plastic roof, creating a blue mist where
the dust motes floated silver and gold like grains of sand
in a stream. Bert had helped Gramp build the carport
onto the single garage. He had been the one to climb the
ladder and nail down the four-by-eight plastic panels.

Bert hit the kill button, and for a second all he
could hear was the exhaust note ringing in his ears. The
screen door opened and Bert's grandmother leaned her
head out. She was in the sunlight there, and her tightly
permed, smoky-blue hair shone as distinctly as if it radiated a light of its own. Bert saw her mouth move, but he
didn't hear a thing. He dismounted and walked out of the
blue mist and into the sunlight.

"Has that motorcycle made you deaf already, Berty?"
Edith Bowden yelled into her grandson's face. She mis-
took the old half-helmet Shepard had lent him for a
Nazi helmet she'd seen on a TV biker. "You look like a
German," she said.

Bert stood on the sidewalk and his grandmother stood on the porch step, which put them face-to-face. Bert smiled at the *irked* expression she wore. It was her word and it always made Bert smile. Almost everything about Gram made him smile. He took off the helmet and set it on one of the thin white trellis staves where the moss-rose vines hadn't woven themselves. He'd helped Gramp make the trellis, too.

"What's that, Gram?" Bert said. "Can't hear very well. Think the bike's made me deaf. Really irks me."

"Such a noise could make a person deaf," she replied. "I don't know why that thing isn't against the law."

In terms of noise level it probably is, Bert thought. "I just stopped by to remind you I love you," he said. "And to create an irksome racket with my motorcycle."

"You've been to visit your grandfather," she said. "You always stop by to remind me you love me when you've been to visit your grandfather."

"I don't think he hears me when I tell him," Bert said. He was surprised to hear himself say this. It wasn't something he would have said if he'd thought about it first.

Edith Bowden put a hand on her grandson's shoulder and stepped down onto the sidewalk. "Berty," she said, "you told him often enough when he could hear you."

And then Bert was crying, which surprised him as much as what he'd just said. He broke out into big, gaspy sobs. Tears filled his eyes, brimmed over, ran down his cheeks and dropped off his chin. Snot collected on his upper lip in a gray moustache, and he wiped it off with the back of his hand.

Edith held Bert's arm and walked him a few steps across the grass to an addition built perpendicular to the garage. It looked like a tiny house with its chimney, wide windows, curtains, and window box still blooming geraniums, but it was a workshop. She nudged Bert into a seat on the red wooden bench under the window box. In her mind she could see her Bert and little Berty hanging the window box, painting the bench. She pulled a tissue from her apron pocket and held it out.

It embarrassed Bert to be bawling with such gusto. Weeping of this or any sort didn't fit with the biker image he would like to cultivate. It didn't integrate into the music of power, which was the sound a Harley made. But, God, did it feel good just to sit there and wail. His whole body gave in to it. It was like falling asleep when he couldn't stay awake another second. He took the tissue from Gram and wiped his nose. She sat down beside him and patted his leg.

Bert looked over at the little pink house where his grandparents had lived for ten years, where his grandmother now lived alone. The living room couch folded out, and he had slept many nights there after whirling the last old maid through the buttery grit at the bottom of the popcorn bowl and crunching it, after wrestling or bowling or a wildlife show had ended at ten. He breathed deep and slow, blew his nose, looked down at the ragged tissue. He'd told himself he was riding over here to be a comfort to his grandmother, but he guessed he was really here for the comfort she and Gramp had always given him.

Chapter 13

Lucky Bert Bowden

Bert gave a hand signal as he turned north on Division. He checked both mirrors and signaled again before he slipped into the right lane. *You can count on drivers of cars to be predictable in one sense only,* Shepard had told him. *They'll always be dangerous. They'll look right at you, their faces will even seem to acknowledge you, then they'll pull out, anyway.* Bert was being particularly careful because he was breaking the law riding without the company of a licensed rider. Riding a motorcycle on Division during rush hour was unwise, and it was grossly stupid when you didn't even have your operator's license. Bert knew this, but he was riding, anyway.

Traffic moved about forty-five miles an hour, and it was bumper-to-bumper. Bumper-to-bumper, that is, unless you were on a motorcycle, in which case you had no bumper. You had tires, fenders, a helmet, your skull— but you had no bumper.

Bert watched the Blazer in front, the cars moving on both sides, and he checked his mirrors for encroachment from the rear. They might get him, but they wouldn't take him by surprise.

He insinuated himself into the right lane a long ways

before the turn to Shepard's, and he rode close to the curb
to keep plenty of distance between him and the cars nosing
over into any little space that opened up. From the middle
lane a guy about Bert's dad's age in a brown jacked-up
Ford 4x4 looked at him. The guy seemed to see Bert. He
even stretched his neck to look back as he cut over into
Bert's lane. The cab of the pickup fit fine into the space
between Bert and the red Miata in front, but there was no
place for the rest of it.

This happened too fast for Bert to yell at the guy or to
have hit the horn button. Neither of these efforts would
have helped, anyway, because the guy's truck was louder
than Bert's bike. The whir of his oversized, all-terrain tires
alone was enough to drown out the Sportster. What Bert
did was exactly what he should have done: He gassed it
and shot up over the curb.

It was lucky for Bert and the people in the world who
loved him that he hit the curb at just the right angle to go
over it rather than skitter along the edge where the pickup
would have caught him and where some part of him would
have ended up under its right rear tire.

Lucky Bert Bowden straddled the idling Sportster in
the nursery parking lot and screamed after the Ford-man
with all his might, "You cocksucker!" He closed his eyes
and took a deep breath, and then he heard a familiar voice.

"You've had that bike what—twenty-four hours? And
already you're talkin' like a biker. Who says the American
teenager ain't a fast learner?"

There stood Scott Shepard holding a coffee can full of straw flowers. "How come you're not at football practice?" he said. "Camille told me you're a QB."

"I got cut," Bert said. "I'm not a QB anymore." Bert was amazed that Camille knew his name.

"That's too bad," Shepard said. "Shut that thing down and we'll walk back to the shop. You might need a place to change your shorts."

Shepard bounced the can of flowers against his leg as they walked to the alley. He actually limped on both legs. Bert had never seen anyone limp on both legs before.

"Easy to get hurt on a motorcycle," Shepard said. "Easiest thing in the world. Especially for an inexperienced—and I might add an unlicensed—young shitball such as yourself."

"I know," Bert said. "I know." He was smiling at the way Shepard had called him a shitball.

Shepard pointed at Bert's Reeboks. "You know?" he said. "You don't know much or you wouldn't be riding in basketball shoes. Guy needs a decent pair of boots if he's gonna ride a motorcycle.

"There'll come a time when one of those laces catches around your shifter or your brake pedal," Shepard said. "If you need to stop fast, you'll be in trouble because the only brake you'll be able to get to is the front, and on these old bastards the front brake ain't enough. Say you do get stopped and you go to put your foot down to steady the bike. Your foot's not gonna reach the ground because your shoelace is caught. You're already leaning the bike and you've got no leverage to stop it, so you and the bike go over. Besides looking a fool, which nobody ever died from, you break a bunch of shit on the bike and maybe on yourself, or maybe somebody just drives over you."

Bert looked down as he pushed the bike. The loops of his shoelaces were four inches long. Maybe longer.

"And let's say this," Shepard went on. "Let's say you're whipping along through traffic on Division here, and those laces are flapping around and one of 'em gets caught in the chain. Ever see a section of highway where a deer or a big dog got hit? How there's that one big splatter and then smaller and smaller spots down the road?"

Bert saw bright blood shining. He nodded his head.

"They'd collect your pieces in a plastic bag," Shepard said. "Your folks would get a call, they'd go, and that's the last they'd see of their boy."

Shepard stopped. He bent and set the flowers on the asphalt, then pulled up one leg of his jeans. Bert looked at the boot. It had a strap where laces would be. He saw Shepard's pale, hairy leg. Then he saw his grandfather's leg. Then he saw the blood again.

"People call these motorcycle boots," Shepard said. "But they're engineer boots. Their function is not to stomp heads, but to protect feet. As you can see, they have no laces to catch on something and end your days." He snugged the leg of his jeans over the boot, picked up his flowers, and headed down the alley again.

"Is that what happened to your legs?" Bert asked.

"No," Shepard replied. "One knee went in football, and the other in an accident in my job."

Up ahead Bert saw Shepard's partner spraying off an old bike. He was wearing sunglasses and looked so much like Billy Gibbons of ZZ Top that Bert wouldn't have been surprised to see him pull a V-shaped guitar from behind the trash barrel and whip into "Legs" or "Sleeping Bag."

Shepard held the dried flowers above his head as he walked through the mist thrown up by the pressure sprayer.

Bert slowed to have a look at the old bike. Dave didn't look up from the rear wheel where he was directing the nozzle.

The sprocket, hub, and wheel rim were so thick with grease that no metal showed through. Dirty white feathers clung to the grease, and Bert wondered if a chicken had tried to cross the road at the wrong moment back when this poor old wreck had been a running motorcycle.

The hiss died and Dave turned and extended his big, wet hand. "I see both you and the old Sportster are still in one piece," he said.

"Barely," Bert replied.

"Stay off your head, youngster," Dave said, and he turned back to his work.

Bert pushed the Sportster out of the mist and parked it to one side of the open overhead door Shepard had entered. He took off his mist-covered glasses and wiped them on his T-shirt.

A wooden shed ran the length of the cinder-block building. The door of the shed was open. Bert peeked in and his eyes went big. Old motorcycles leaned one against the other, packed tight as anchovies in a can, from the sun-lit doorway into the darkness at the end of the shed. The chrome and rust cast a dull sheen and made Bert imagine gold shining through the dust of years. The air was thick with the smell of old grease and rubber gone to rot, and he caught a whiff of leather.

The next thing Bert caught was a hot, hard jab above his right kidney. He gasped and threw up his arms.

"You've seen our stash," the voice said. "Now we'll have t' waste ya."

It wasn't Shepard and it wasn't his partner.

"Turn around," the voice said.

Bert turned. It was the biker who had come to football practice with Shepard, the guy who wanted to beat up Coach Christman, the guy with the big arms, the guy who didn't need big arms because he carried a gun, the guy Bert had called the police on. He held the sprayer level with Bert's chin.

"You the kid bought the Sportster?"

Bert nodded.

"World's best buy on a motorcycle," the guy said. "We'll have to let you live. Thanks to your acuity and decisiveness, there'll be a hot tub on the Shepard estate.

I myself plan to be the first Shepard soothed in its balmy effervescence. I may have to fight my brother and my nephew for the honor," he said. "But I'm up to it." He extended his hand. "Steve Shepard."

Bert lowered his arms. "Bert Bowden," he said as he shook hands. He wanted to smile, but he wasn't sure it would be prudent.

"Bert," Steve said, "I want you to experience something of the sensation your purchase will bring to others." He lowered the sprayer and blasted Bert in the chest.

It was just one pull of the trigger, just a quick squirt that left a latitudinal line through the word "Shepard's." It startled Bert, though, and he stumbled back into the shed like he'd been shot. He fell against an old bike's front fender.

Steve tossed the sprayer in the air, the red hose trailing like a piece of intestine.

Dave caught it above his head.

"Billy Gibbons!" Steve said. "I knew it was you. I just needed to see that guitar in your hand."

Steve turned to Bert. "Guy here probably introduced himself as Dave Ward, right?" He didn't wait for Bert to respond. "Actually this is old Billy Gibbons, famed ax-man for ZZ Top. Does bikes when he's not on the road with the band. But then a pup like yourself wouldn't know ZZ Top."

Bert wanted to say he'd seen Dave's resemblance to Billy Gibbons right away, but he didn't.

"Let me guess," Steve said. "Your favorite song stylist is . . ." He closed his eyes, dipped his head, and put his fingers to his temples. In a few seconds he raised his head and made a face that suggested enlightenment. "Tiffany!" he proclaimed.

Barfola, Bert wanted to say.

But Bert couldn't have gotten a word in because Steve went right on talking. "Big Billy Gibbons!" he said. "How 'bout a tune?"

Dave held the pressure wand like a guitar. "This'n goes out to Steve Shepard," he said. Then he leveled the wand and let fly.

"Mama!" Steve yelled as he ran into the shop. "Mama!"

Bert walked back into the sunlight. He looked at Dave smiling and holding the wand nozzle-down, leaning on it like a cane. "You'd think that man was on drugs," he said.

No shit, Bert thought. He nodded his head.

"But he ain't," Dave said. "It's just Shepard juice, I guess. Scotty's like that too when you get him goin'. The difference with Steve is he's goin' all the time."

Steve was behind the counter drying off with a shop rag when Bert looked in from the work area. Scotty waved from the showroom where he stood with two uniformed Spokane cops by the custom Harleys. "Catalog's on the counter," he said. "Steve'll ride with you to buy some boots."

Steve tossed Bert an L.L. Bean catalog. It was what Bert had come for.

Bert and Steve rumbled down Division like a mobile earthquake, like a volcanic eruption. When they stopped for a light on the way back from Sears, Bert felt the pavement vibrating through the soles of his new boots. They rolled down the alley behind the nursery and stopped in back of the shop. Bert hit his kill button, but Steve kept his bike running. He stretched out his arm and Bert saw the shoulder holster under his sleeveless jean jacket. "I'll see ya, Bootsie," he said.

Bert didn't realize at first that Steve wanted to shake hands. He was holding his forearm upward, and when Bert reached to shake in the traditional way Steve hooked his thumb, turned his palm perpendicular to Bert's, and held him in the grip that symbolizes fraternity. Steve pumped Bert's hand twice, then let go. "I want you not only to stay off your head," Steve said over the roar of the engine, "I want none of your body parts except your feet in those new boots to touch the pavement."

"Thanks for riding with me," Bert replied.

"We'll do 'er again," Steve said. Then he was off down the alley.

Bert turned and saw Scotty standing in the doorway. "Come in and have a sit," he said.

Bert settled into the old chair next to the wood stove. This back corner with the old Coke machine, stove, couch, chair, floor lamp, and the old console radio was like a living room from the World War II era. The only modern thing here was the big Ektelon gym bag sitting beside the chair. Racquetball gloves hung from the carrying straps. Some were new and soft-looking, but most were old, sweat-stained and brittle like animal skins run over and rained on so many times the fur is gone. Through the open zipper Bert saw a blue ball lying against a white weave of racquet strings. Bert had never played racquetball. He wondered how Scotty could play with such bad knees.

"The restoration business requires some research," Scotty said. "Even guys like Dave and I who've been working on these bikes most of our lives have to do a lot of reading. So we've got the couch and chair and the lamp. This stuff came from the house Steve and I grew up in."

Bert wondered what kind of kids became men like Scott and Steve Shepard.

"You play a winter sport?" Scotty asked.

"I played basketball in grade school," Bert replied. "I don't play anything anymore."

"There's a job open here after school and Saturdays," Scotty said. "It runs from now till the end of basketball season. I was saving it for my boy, but he surprised us and made the football team. It's dirty work mostly—cleaning bikes and parts. After a while, if you decide you like being around a shop, we'll teach you how to tune and service."

"I'll take it," Bert said.

"Think about it," Scotty said. "Talk it over with your folks and let me know tomorrow."

Bert didn't need to think about it, and he didn't want to talk it over with his folks. But "Okay" was what he said.

Shepard stood and Bert stood. Bert extended his hand and they shook in the traditional way.

Bert was about to bring his weight down on the kick pedal when the growl of an engine made him stop and turn. It had sounded like a bike, but it was a sports car with a blond woman at the wheel. Bert turned back to his business, wound up, and came down on the pedal. In the mirror he saw Scotty walk to the car with the can of flowers. Bert was curious to see more, but he'd come to the end of the alley and it was time to head for home.

Bert lay in bed knowing it had been a lucky day and that he was a lucky guy. If he'd made the football team, he wouldn't have a job at Shepard's Classic and Custom, and he'd rather work there than be a third-string quarterback.

He wondered how they could have doubted Camille would make the team. The kid was as big as his dad. A guy would have a lot better chance of being somebody, Bert thought, if he evolved out of the Shepard gene pool.

Bert hated it that he wanted so much and that he envied what other people had. He knew he was more fortunate than most of the people in the world. He had his own room in a nice house, a sound system, a TV, his own phone, he was healthy, and he owned not one but two motor vehicles. Bert knew he was a lucky guy.

Chapter 14

"Though Much Is Taken, Much Abides"

Thompson High's first pep convocation of the year is in its initial phase of combustion. The auditorium is packed with clapping, chanting students. There's a football game tonight and volleyball tomorrow night. The football boys sit on folding chairs on one side of the stage, and the volleyball girls sit on the other. Bert Bowden, who is not burning with the flame of school spirit, sits in the darkness in the last row of the upper level. Up here he doesn't feel the urge to stand when everybody stands, clap when everybody claps, yell when everybody yells.

Bert likes the pep cons. He finds them fascinating, and high in the darkness he can be fascinated in peace. There's always a trade-off, of course. In this case Bert is trading the inspiration he feels at watching kids root for other kids who are trying to be somebody against the desperation he feels at being nobody. At being worse than nobody, really. At being too small-hearted to stand up and cheer with the rest of the crowd for people who have earned the acclaim and deserve the boost.

Bert wishes he were up on the stage with the varsity

football team now. But he's not and he knows he doesn't deserve to be. He does, however, yearn for a seat on some stage sometime somewhere.

Coach Christman has risen to introduce the football team. Bert would rather listen to something else, so he pulls from his back pocket the essay Tanneran returned this morning, squints into the darkness, and reads the man's comments one more time.

Bert,

You're a good writer. Your prose doesn't sound like writing, or like someone straining to sound like a writer. The voice is of a thoughtful person talking, and that's exactly what it needs to be.

One of your strongest qualities as a writer, it seems to me, is your ability first to see, and then to remember and use the sensory details that focus your readers' attention in a scene.

You say, for example, "Ours was an old school with wooden floors, and some of the boards had warped at the edges and were no longer level with the others. I felt the metal legs of the desk-chair catch on these raised boards and rip through them. The room was silent except for the squeal of the metal legs of my desk sliding over the floor and the intermittent splintering of the board edges."

This is good narrative writing, Bert. It does one of the things all good narrative does: It forces the reader to experience what's happening. You take us to that room with you and make us hear your chair go squealing across the floor. You create images in our heads not just of the chair ripping wood, but of the sight of the splintered boards. You don't have to show us those boards specifically because you've already switched on our imaginations, and in our imaginations we see (and hear and smell and touch) the experience ourselves.

You also force us to experience the damage a lousy teacher—maybe good-intentioned, but nevertheless lousy—can do to a kid. This guy took a lot away from you, Bert. But I want you to remember this little line from a great poem: "Though much is taken, much abides." Some of your spirit was taken, yes. But there's plenty left. I see it in your writing, and I know it's still there inside you. And I know you'll find it.

In closing, a demand and an invitation: I demand that you feel good about this piece. It's fine work.

It's the absolute real thing. And I want to invite you
to write for *The Explorer*. If you think you'd enjoy it,
come see me.

Gene Tanneran

Bert is still a little light-headed from this praise. The
feeling has diminished since this morning, and it never was
the dizzying rush he'd feel sitting up on the stage. But it
feels good.

Bert wonders if he'd be up there on stage if so much
had not been taken. He also wonders if much abides.
Sometimes he wonders if there are any positive qualities
left in him at all. Tanneran was kind to say so, but that
doesn't make it true.

The thought of other kids reading his writing is scary.
But it's also alluring. Bert would like to write for the paper.
Is the possibility of recognition worth the risk of ridicule?
That's the question he'll have to answer.

Chapter 15

Peckered

The writing Bert did for *The Explorer* **wasn't much** fun. He did, however, like opening a new ink-smelling paper and finding his byline. He'd scan each page with care, and when he saw his name his chest would go tight for a second. His stories were informative and clear, which is all they were supposed to be. He'd written about tennis, cross-country, junior varsity football, and the new horticulture club. Bert wasn't contemptuous of news writing. He liked the symmetry of the inverted-pyramid style that required the most important element in the lede and elements of declining importance below.

Bert wrote his stories at home after work, and he would not have wanted anyone to find out how long these short, simple pieces took him to complete. It was tough to come up with the right words. When he found the right words, it was tough to get them into sentences that flowed smoothly, then into paragraphs that broke from one another at logical junctures. It was tough to get all the words together so they fit. This was why Bert couldn't believe Tanneran's comment that he was a good writer. If he was good, how come it took him so long to write a sentence?

The writing Bert enjoyed most was what he did for Tanneran's class. Bert did no homework but English. He knew he should, but he just didn't feel like it. There was too much other stuff going on in his life. There had been, for example, his motorcycle-riding exam to deal with.

Bert Bowden

Junior English

October 4, 1989

PECKERED

My boss, Scott Shepard, proprietor of Shepard's Classic and Custom Cycles, warned me that the State Patrol had it in for Harley riders.

"They're pricks to anybody rides a Harley," Scotty said. "Doesn't matter what the guy looks like or how he comports himself. J. Edgar Hoover comes back from the dead and rides through the state of Washington on a Harley, these guys would bust his bulldog jowls from the Idaho border to Puget Sound."

"Only two living beings more contemptuous of Harley riders than your basic Washington State Trooper," Scotty's brother Steve said from beside me where he sat on his idling Harley. "One is a Washington State Trooper who has drawn out-of-state vehicle inspection duty and meets a Harley rider bringing his bike in from California and applying for a Washington title. Those inspections are like a Red Cross search for tainted blood. They check every orifice in the bike and in the owner right down to the exhaust port. Officious pricks," Steve said. "Real peckers. And thorough."

Steve looks like a bad biker, a 1 percenter as they are referred to, but he's not.

I was mounted on my '69 Sportster as this conversation took place. It was a comfort to me that the Sportster was titled in Washington when I bought it from Scotty.

"Another person nastier is a Washington State Trooper monitoring the riding segment of the motorcycle operator's exam," Scotty said. "They can hear a Harley a mile away in heavy traffic. They have recognition of the exhaust note implanted. They hear the H-D, grab an exam sheet, and mark down a failure. They fill in your name after you've rolled in."

I was on my way to take my exam, so this was not good news.

Scotty reached out with the breaker bar he was holding and touched me on the forearm where I wish I had a tattoo but lack the courage. Not the courage to be tattooed, but the courage to face my mom and dad after it's done.

Scotty, Steve, and Scotty's son, Camille, each has a tattoo on his forearm that says RIDE FAST, LIVE FOREVER. My intellect tells me this is a stupid sentiment, but I confess that sometimes when I'm riding and I say it to myself my heart wants to fly out of my chest.

"Let me amend that, Bert," Scotty said. "There's one person a Harley guy can run into who transcends a Washington State Trooper in terms of pure malevolence. That is a female trooper on any duty whatsoever. They are the meanest things under the brim of a hat. They're tough as badgers and their numbers are proliferating." He pointed the bar at Steve. "That correct, Brother?"

"I'd hate to tangle with one," Steve replied. He turned to me, blipped his throttle once, then let it idle down again before he

spoke. "They pride themselves on their knowledge of primitive cir-
cumcision techniques, Bootsie," he said. "We're talking blunt rock
and mussel shell." He gassed it again and was off.

Scotty raised the breaker bar to the bill of his cap. "Good luck,"
he said. "If you pass, take yourself a nice long ride. Don't came
back till after lunch."

Steve and I rode south on Division through the Saturday
morning traffic. As we neared the examining station he slowed. I
rolled into the driveway and stopped to wait for him, but he sat on
his bike in the middle of the street, smiling.

I heard a scuffing on the asphalt and turned. It was a trooper.
A woman. She was striding toward me like a power lifter approach-
ing the bar. She looked like the woman Marine in Aliens. She was
smiling. I guess I was the only one of us not having a good time.

I looked back at Steve. He'd raised and lowered his hand, and
now he was wheeling back toward Division. I'd turned a little too
late to catch his gesture. He might have been giving me a good-bye
wave, but I was afraid he'd been flipping the trooper the bird. She
touched my shoulder.

"Ready to take this old sled through the cones?" she said. Her
name tag read TROOPER HARRISON. "Scotty called and told us
Steve was bringing you down," she said. She looked at her clipboard. "Bert Bowden?"

I nodded.

The test was short and simple. I rode straight along a line
of cones, swerved through another line of cones, banked around
one final cone, accelerated through the gears, then clamped on the
binders for an emergency stop.

Trooper Harrison extended her hand and I took the sheet. At the top she'd written 92%.

I felt weightless as I blazed north on Division. It was tough to hold it at forty. It's always tough to stay close to the speed limit, but it was tougher that morning. The power gets inside you. It's the only sensation I know like listening to good rock and roll. If rock and roll were a machine, it would be a motorcycle.

I watched my reflection flash past in the store windows. I admired the look. Brown leather jacket open over a white T-shirt, old faded jeans, sensible boots. It was a look of confidence. This young dude was evolved. Too bad he wasn't me.

Any other time I would have been brought down by this realization, but on this day I wasn't.

Soon the stores thinned out, the pines began, and Division Street became Highway 395. When I saw the 55 sign I cut loose. It was literally like taking flight. I couldn't hold back. The speedo needle was bouncing off seventy. The wind was pushing my helmet back so hard, my chin strap had begun to strangle me. This was not how a guy stays off his head.

I was up to eighty when I passed the old gravel pit where the highway slopes down to the Little Spokane River. I had to back off then because cars were stopped waiting for a hay truck turning onto the river road. When I reached the intersection I had slowed enough for my good sense to catch me. I gave my hand signal and turned into the cool shadows of the cliffs.

It was sweet riding along the river. There was traffic, but no one was in a hurry. Just cruising. Families. Boyfriends and girlfriends.

Every bike I met carried a couple. The girls were clasped onto the guys like enraptured mollusks onto rocks. This made me aware that I was alone, but it didn't spoil the good time I was having.

I had taken my eyes off the road directly in front of me, but I don't think I would have seen it, anyway. It came too fast. What I did see was a dark blur, and then I felt the impact.

It was like being punched in the sternum by a sharp little fist. It took my breath away for an instant, but it didn't knock the wind out of me. I looked down and saw a bird stuck in my chest.

A big bird. The thing went a good twelve inches from its head to the end of its tail feathers. I couldn't tell about the beak because it was buried to the hilt in my chest. It was long enough to anchor the bird's body flopping against my T-shirt where my jacket hung open. The bird's neck was broken. It was all black except for the white iris of the eyes. Both the black pupil and white iris were opaque. They looked like porcelain.

I maintained an excellent view of the bird even while I was still riding because the thing was four inches from my chin. To oncoming motorists the bird must have looked like a pendant I was wearing. If I'd seen me coming down the road, I'd have said, "Now there's a dude with some arcane jewelry!"

I pulled off at a litter barrel, took hold of the bird's warm body, and yanked. It slipped right out. It felt funny, but I wouldn't say it hurt. I watched the white cotton cloth of my T-shirt absorb the blood. The spot didn't grow bigger than a quarter. The bird's beak was about an inch and a half long and shaped like a little chisel. It was some kind of woodpecker.

I lifted a ketchup-stained Arby's bag out of the barrel, deposited the bird, then replaced the bag. I zipped up my coat and headed back to town with tetanus on my mind.

Back at the shop I told Scotty about being drilled by a woodpecker. He enjoyed it. He said the troopers let me slide, but I'd wound up getting peckered, anyway.

Chapter 16

The Most Important Thing
to Do with Bert Bowden

Gene Tanneran reads the concluding line of "Peckered," Bert Bowden's personal narrative, and smiles. He nods his head, drops the stapled pages onto his kitchen table, and gets to his feet.

It's a quarter past midnight and time for high school English teachers to put away their pens. *Slow Train Comin'* floats in from the living room, and Tanneran smiles again as he pours the last of the coffee and shuts off the pot. A piece of student writing made him forget Dylan was on the stereo. Such a powerful diversion doesn't take place every night. He will write Bert a note and hit the hay.

Tanneran knows that the most important thing to do with Bert Bowden is just to like him. Bert doesn't send many signals out into the world, but the ones he does send are going to reflect back to him off Gene Tanneran with the message "Bert Bowden, you are a neat guy." Which is nothing more than the truth.

Tanneran feels an almost personal shame that a member of his profession spent two years creating a world where Bert's reflection showed him he was shit.

Tanneran will give Bert specific criticism of his work,

of course. He will recommend books to read, he will encourage, he will suggest to Darby Granger, the paper's editor, that she assign Bert a feature story so his writing skills are challenged. Tanneran will help all he can. But the most important thing he can do with Bert is like him. Massive doses of affection. Once the kid begins to feel like he deserves success, he'll start creating some.

Bert is easy to like. Most of the kids are. But Tanneran can't like them all. He wishes he knew some exercise to create a more loving heart. He has begun to feel his store of affection grow leaner with each passing year. In his twenties he couldn't imagine a bottom to the well from which his energy, tolerance, and affection flowed. In his thirties he felt that power diminish. Now, in his forties, he's often forced to dip deep. He doesn't see a way in the world he can keep teaching high school until he's old enough to retire. He even prays for Christian love to transform him. He remains, however, untransformed. So he does the best he can: He pretends.

Tanneran treats all the kids as though he likes them. Even the most contemptible little assholes. His hope is that this exercise will get his heart back into shape.

The thing that Tanneran believes to be his greatest success as a teacher isn't mentioned in his personnel file. No one knows about it. Every time Tanneran calls Rick Curtis's name and Curtis only nods, every time he asks him a question and Curtis doesn't respond, every time he looks at the kid's face with its permanent sneer and does not unleash a spray of sarcasm over the self-deluded little prick like a burst of toxic chemicals, does not grab his guitar and bash him in the head with it, every time Tanneran does not give in to the lure of such pleasure, it is a victory.

Tanneran knows that Curtis has a shitty home life, knows the kid's superiority is just a pose, is pretty sure he refuses to answer questions not because he has a disdain for school, as he and his little coterie would like people to believe, but because he has an undiagnosed learning disability. Tanneran knows, in fact, that Rick Curtis needs affection and encouragement as bad as Bert Bowden. But he hates the kid so fiercely, he doesn't give a fuck.

Tanneran will not, however, add his message to all the other messages in Curtis's life that tell him he's no good. Tanneran will continue to practice affection on Rick Curtis and others in spite of how he feels about them. When he can't be decent to the kids he doesn't like, that's when he'll quit teaching.

Chapter 17

Term of Endearment

When Bert considers Darby Granger objectively, as he is doing now from across the journalism room, he is forced to admit that she doesn't have the perfect body. Her breasts are a little small, her butt a little big. Bert wonders if it is to deemphasize the breadth of her hips that she so often wears loose, wide-waisted jeans. You can look at her butt in those jeans and not even notice that the Darb is a minor pudge.

She is not wearing jeans today, however. Today it's baggy boxers, a baggy white T-shirt, and a baggy blue blazer.

Darby doesn't have big hair that retains a wet look throughout the day and makes her appear to be exceeding the speed limit in a vintage convertible when she is in fact not moving at all. That is to say, she hasn't modeled her coiffure on women in beer commercials and cigarette ads. Her hair is short, dark brown, curly. She wears round gold wire-rim glasses, no earrings, and no makeup that Bert has been able to detect, unless she uses a blush formula that mimics the mild glow of windburn.

There's a softness in Darby's appearance and a contrasting strength in her manner. And she's real smart. Bert has heard her do surgery on the staff with her sarcasm, such scorching commentaries having earned her the nickname Darb Vader. She doesn't seem to need people to think she's smart, though. She doesn't seem to need people to think she's anything, except editor of *The David Thompson Explorer*, and this strength is more alluring to Bert than muscle tone. Bert has suffered thoughts of Darby since the morning he first saw her in the journalism room and didn't know her name.

Bert would like Darby to know that Tanneran thinks he's a good writer. He's considering walking around the table and letting his essay slip out of his back pocket next to Darby's grapes and cheese. When she returns from talking to the photographers, she might notice Tanneran's hand-writing and get curious. But this is too weasely a thing for even the weasely Bert Bowden.

And it's also too late, because Darby is crossing the floor right now. Bert lowers his eyes to the last half of his sandwich. His peripheral vision just includes Darby's green grapes across the table. He keeps his eyes at this angle as he takes a bite of sandwich, the totality of his manner meant to illustrate the hypnotic appeal of peanut butter, honey, and his grandmother's homemade bread. Bert chews and watches Darby's grapes. Darby does not appear behind them. Bert feels a presence at his side.

"Bowden?" the voice says.

Bert turns to face Darby's boxer shorts. As he raises his eyes a viscous brown string descends from his sandwich to the chest of his white T-shirt where the word TRIUMPH is written in blue over a picture of an old Triumph twin. He tilts the sandwich and puts it back down on the table. He looks at the brown doodle on his shirt. He looks up at Darby, who is looking down at him.

"Nasty sandwich," she says. She squinches her face. "That looks like something my baby sister . . . Never mind," she says.

With his finger Bert scrapes off what he can of the sticky stuff. Then he licks the finger.

Darby squinches her face again. "Bowden," she says, "Tanneran thinks you're a good writer, and he'd like to see you do a feature for us. I had an idea that might interest you."

She steps around the table, grabs her chair with one hand and the paper towel her lunch is sitting on with the other, and slides both nearer Bert. She sits down and pops a grape into her mouth.

"There's a French kid in my English class," Darby says. "Among other things, he's into motorcycles. He's also on the football team. To be perfectly honest," she says, "he's a stud muffin." She points a cheese stick at Bert's shirt. "You're into motorcycles, and I thought you might like to profile him for us."

"That's Camille Shepard," Bert replies. "I work for his dad." A voice in Bert's head is telling him to be cool, not to present even the slightest suggestion that he needs this. "I could give it a try," he says.

Darby rises and waves the Asian kid over. "Bert

Bowden," she says, "this is Cheng Moua. He's a member of the Hmong ethnic group, and he's the photographer you'll work with. Read my lips," she says. "Cheng Moua, not Eddie Hmongster."

As Bert rises to shake Cheng's extended hand, Mark Schwartz, seated on the window ledge, chants, "Hmongster! Hmongster! Hmongster!"

"Shut up, Schwartz, you gonad," Darby says.

"Hi, Bert," Cheng says. "Call me Eddie if you want."

Before Bert can reply, Darby says, "Cheng is the only photographer we have who can shoot thirty-six exposures without thirty of them featuring Krista James."

"I have exposed Krista many times," Schwartz says. "On the volleyball court and other places. It was good for both of us."

As Darby faces Bert and Cheng, Schwartz makes masturbation gestures.

Darby turns and catches Schwartz with his hand in midstroke. He pretends that his hand is a camera and brings the other hand up to capture the moment. "And now, Darb Vader," Schwartz says. "I have exposed you."

Darby shakes her head as she turns back to Cheng and Bert. "I've been trying to recruit some female photographers since school started," she says.

"So have I," Schwartz says.

Darby doesn't acknowledge this. Cheng says he's got film in the bath and jogs back to the darkroom. Darby moves to sit, so Bert sits too. But then Darby does not sit, and Bert is eye level with the neatly sewn stitches that hem the portal in her paisley-patterned boxers. He wonders if she's wearing panties under there. And what's that fragrance? Is it . . . ? Oh, God, it's baby powder!

Bert's throat begins to constrict. His mass goes critical. He will melt down if he doesn't disengage. He drops his head to the table with a turgid thunk.

Darby turns and looks down. "You're a strange one, Bowden," she says. "You might be a good writer, but I think you are also an egg."

Great, Bert thinks. Camille Shepard is a stud muffin and I'm an egg. He opens his eyes and watches Darby's hands wrap up her grapes and cheese. He watches her boxers move toward the door.

"I had you pegged for an egg," says Darby. "A reticent egg." And then she's gone.

The Hmongster sits down in Darby's chair. "She called you a *resident egg?*" he asks.

Bert raises his head. *"Reticent,"* he replies. "Reserved, hesitant to speak out."

"She's right," the Hmongster says. "These are the first words I've heard you say."

"It also refers to a guy with some really ugly shit in his hair," Schwartz says as he points toward Bert's right ear.

Bert reaches and finds the goo. He rises and heads for the door. "Be right back," he says. "Please don't eat my sandwich."

"Don't worry," the Hmongster says.

"Looks like it already passed through that stage of the nourishment process," Schwartz says.

Bert walks to the bathroom with a smile on his face. He gets a kick out of the Hmongster and Schwartz. And to his peanut-butter-and-honey-covered ear, *reticent egg* has begun to ring like a term of endearment.

Chapter 18

Camille Shepard Embraces His Father

Bert saw Jim Zimster sitting in his wheelchair on the front porch of a house a couple blocks away from the stadium. This was the second time he'd seen him sitting there on the evening of a football game, and the thought flashed: What if he'd like to go but doesn't have a ride? Bert couldn't take him on the Sportster, but he slowed, anyway, as he watched Jim sitting in the yellow glow of his porch light.

Bert was so absorbed he didn't hear the rumble of the engine behind him. When the horn went off a few feet from his rear fender he almost lost control. He pulled to the curb and took a couple deep breaths. When no car went by, Bert looked behind him. There was the Shepard's Classic and Custom van idling in front of Zimster's house. Zimster was rolling down the sidewalk, and Scotty was waiting for him at the back of the van.

Bert waved and Scotty waved. Rita Dixon, Scotty's girlfriend, waved from the passenger seat. Bert was amazed that Zimster waved too. Scotty pulled two motorcycle ramps out of the van and set them the width of Jim's wheels. Bert thought about helping, but Scotty had Jim up in the van before Bert could climb off his bike. Bert waved again and headed for the stadium wondering how Zimster knew the Shepards.

The Explorer varsity was five-and-five going into their game with the Rogers Pirates. Camille Shepard had played only a few downs late in games with the outcome already decided. Bert had interviewed him twice for the profile, and he was about ready to put it together. He just wanted to watch one more game.

Camille had said it was great just being on the team, but Bert could tell it hurt him not to play. At least Bert thought he could tell that. Something had been in the big kid's voice and in his eyes that hadn't been in his words.

It was Rats 27–Explorers 7 with less than a minute to go in the third quarter and the Explorer receiving team taking the field when Coach Heslin walked up to Coach Christman, said something, and then looked toward the bench. Christman yelled, "Shepard!" and Camille came running.

Bert carried a press badge that allowed him on the field, but at the half he'd walked up into the seats to munch some of Rita's popcorn. Rita, Scotty, Zimster, and Steve Shepard sat in the first row of the second level because the walkway there was wide enough for Zimster's chair, which was positioned between Scotty and Steve. Next to Steve sat Mike Jackson's dad, and in the rows behind sat the families of other team members.

When Camille ran onto the field, Steve jumped to his

feet, raised both fists, and yelled, "Yes!" Scotty was a little slower. He yelled, "Go get 'em, Shepard!" Bert saw Eddie Hmongster move up closer to the sideline and raise his camera. Everybody in the Thompson section stood for the kickoff.

Mike Jackson and Camille were deep to receive. It was a high, beautiful kick, and it settled into Mike's hands at the same time eight snarling Rogers Rats were tearing up the Explorer wedge. Mike headed to Camille's side of the field, away from the carnage. But the carnage pursued him, and he hadn't made five yards on his slant when orange jerseys blocked the way. Mike Jackson could take a hit as well as anybody, but he lateraled the ball to Camille.

Shepard would have made a yard or two up the sidelines, which is what everyone including the Rats figured he'd do. But he ran the other way. Not far, just enough to slip past the charging Rats, then he cut straight to the middle of the field.

The Rogers half of the field was nearly deserted. There was only the Rat end converging from the far sideline, and the Rat kicker waiting at the thirty.

The Thompson fans were going crazy. For a moment Bert was blinded by popcorn.

Camille shifted the ball to his right hand as the Rat end bore in on his left. Scotty and Steve looked at each other, then Steve looked down at Zimster. "You might want to hide your eyes, Zim," he said. "This is going to be rated R for violence."

Camille didn't juke, jive, fake, cut, or leap. What he did was time his collision with the end to correspond with the twin explosions upward of his left arm, which he had cocked in the manner of a defensive lineman about to deliver a forearm shiver, and his left knee. The Rogers player went up in the air like a sack of beets leaving the back of a truck. Camille didn't break stride.

The Rogers kicker, a little guy, had an angle on Camille, and he kept his head up all the way to the point of impact. Or he would have if there'd been impact. Camille cut inside just as he was about to make the hit. All the kid hit was air.

In a couple more strides Camille crossed the goal line. He tossed the ball to the ref, then was knocked flat by a flying Mike Jackson. Soon they were both buried in a green-and-gold pile of Thompson players.

Scotty and Steve chanted into each other's faces, "Shepard! Shep-ard!" Zimster howled like a dog. Rita jettisoned the rest of the popcorn. It was a middle-American high school football family madhouse.

The Thompson players finally unpiled and Camille jogged back to the sideline carrying his helmet. When he neared midfield he stopped and looked up at Scotty. Bert had been watching him every step, and he observed this moment isolated from the movement all around. Bert turned and saw Scotty looking down at Camille. What Bert saw pass between the father and son sent a current of emotion through him.

Bert knew there was a story in that look.

"Are you ready for some foot-bawl?" Mr. Jackson sang out as the Thompson kicker waited for the ref's whistle.

The Rats ran a play, then the horn sounded and the teams changed ends. Fourth quarter. Rogers 27, Thompson 14. Plenty of time.

The Rats made a first down, but Thompson held in the next series and Shepard went in to receive the punt. The Rat punter dribbled it about eight yards. Shepard didn't get near it.

The Explorer offense had a new look when they lined up. Shepard at tight end, Kelly McDougall set wide at the other end, Jackson a yard off the line between Kelly-Mac and the tackle in a receiver's position, and Sean Christman at QB.

Mike Jackson Sr. looked at Steve. Steve looked at Scotty. Scotty looked back at both of them. Zimster looked up at everybody but nobody noticed. "Guess they're goin' with the guys with the best hands," Scotty said.

At the snap Christman dropped deep, Shepard ran a sideline left, Kelly-Mac went post left, and Jackson held his block. When the coverage had drifted far enough left, Jackson slid off the block and swung for the right sideline. Christman floated the ball sweet and fat as a pumpkin, Jackson ran under it and kept going to the thirty.

Shepard hooked over the middle and caught a bullet. He was nailed before he could go anywhere, but it was seven yards. Then everybody went deep. Shepard leaped out of the crowd at the goal line, pulled it in, and fell into the end zone.

Jubilation reigned only briefly among the Thompson fans. Both Explorer tackles had also gone deep on the play. Illegal receiver. Fifteen yards in the wrong direction and a loss of the down.

On the next play Christman rolled right in what looked like a sweep. But he reversed the ball to Jackson coming left. Shepard buried the defensive end, and Jackson outran the few Rats who realized he had the ball. Six more for the green and gold. The kick was good. Rogers 27, Thompson 21. Six minutes on the clock.

The Rats got a good runback. Then they ran for three first downs. Then the only place to go was into the Explorer end zone. But the Explorers held one . . . two . . . three downs. And then the Rats kicked a field goal.

"A field goal?" Bert heard Steve say. "What is this? High school kids don't kick field goals."

"That's the seventh the Rogers kid's kicked this season," Zimster said.

"Nobody kicked field goals when we were playin'," Steve said.

"You guys played in leather helmets—right?" Zimster said.

"Right," Steve said. "And we had no modern footballs. We had to rip the larger organs out of our friends and use them." Steve wrapped one arm around Zimster's thin shoulders and placed his other hand at his sternum, flexing his fingers like a claw. "And that, Jimmie the Zim, is what we did to our friends," he said.

"I don't think you'd get a lot of play out of my organs," Jim said. "They weren't made to last."

Steve laughed. He kept his arm around Jim's chair and remained seated for the kickoff.

Pirates 30, Explorers 21. Three minutes.

The same kid who kicked the field goal booted this one into the end zone. Jackson couldn't run it out.

It didn't look like the Explorers could do it, and in this instance appearance coincided with reality: They didn't do it. There was one play, however, that made folks glad they stuck around.

After Christman got sacked on the ten, he hit Kelly-Mac for twelve and Jackson for six. But that was still two short of a first. So it was fourth down and the Explorers were on their own twenty-eight with a minute left. No sense punting.

Christman got the ball on the first hut, flipped it out to Jackson, who had stayed behind the line of scrimmage, then blindsided the linebacker who was bearing down on Mike as though he were a double cheeseburger after the game. Jackson, who can throw the ball from Spokane to the Canadian border, pumped his arm in Kelly-Mac's direction, stopping the rest of the charging Rat linemen. This gave him enough time to wind up and fling one to Shepard, who was streaking down the sideline like the famous French high-speed train.

The two Rat safeties had been camped at midfield, so they were right with Shepard when the ball spiraled over their twenty. Shepard went up and the Rats went up. But Shepard went higher. He went so high, in fact, that the gold number 88 on his green jersey was visible above both Rogers players.

This was the point at which someone might have asked Scotty: Does your kid play basketball? But nobody did.

Shepard grabbed the ball with one hand but wasn't able to pull it in before the three of them landed out of bounds around the ten. Shepard was the first to his feet, and he was holding the ball high.

The referee signaled that the play was no good, that Shepard had caught it out.

Coach Christman exhibited signs of demonic possession. He ran onto the field waving both arms and kicking his legs high in the manner of a Nazi goose step. His clipboard flew into the air higher than Jackson's pass. Heslin grabbed him before he could get to the referee.

Steve, Mr. Jackson, Jimmie the Zim, Rita, and the host of Thompson fans in the seats behind screamed threats, excoriations, and vile expletives. Nobody but Bert heard Scotty say, "I think he was out."

When order was finally restored the ball went to the Rats back at the Explorer twenty-eight. For spite they tried to score, but two passes went incomplete and the gun sounded before they could get off another snap.

There was a great exhalation of coffee- and popcorn-breath out of the Thompson section and then everybody began packing up. Generally spirits were high. People were talking about the potential of this new offensive lineup.

Camille walked up to the concrete wall where the seats began. His hair was matted down and a mixture of field chalk and sod was stuck above one eye. Scotty walked down to meet him. Bert saw this and he saw the Hmongster a few feet away sighting in with the school's Pentax.

"I didn't get control till I was out," Camille said.

"That's what it looked like to me," Scotty said. "Great catch, anyway. Great game.'

Camille beamed. He spotted Zimster up in the crowd and yelled. "Jim! You want to meet us back at school and go cruise for a dog?"

Zimster gave him a thumbs-up.

Bert watched Scotty watch Camille walk down the sideline and then up the asphalt walkway toward the bus.

The mood back at school was such that if Bert hadn't been to the game, he would have thought they'd won. Everybody—guys, girls, the few parents waiting to have a word with their sons before the boys went off into the postgame night where they had a lot better chance of getting hurt in their cars than on the football field— everybody was full of smiles, good cheer, and high hopes for the next game, which would be the last. Band kids, a subspecies defying the usual human classifications, were singing "Twist and Shout" and dancing like the parade crowd in *Ferris Bueller's Day Off*. Some parents carped about Coach Christman not moving Jackson to receiver earlier in the year, but they carped good-naturedly.

It was a beautiful night. A little cool, a little moist. Just right for wearing your hooded sweatshirt under your coat. The players coming out of the locker room didn't seem to want to leave either. They hung around, sitting on the steps or leaning against car fenders.

Bert was looking over at Jim, wondering what had happened to all his nastiness. Jim was sitting in his chair at the rear of Camille's 1949 Chevy station wagon talking with Scotty and Rita. Thinking of Zimster made Bert think about grade school, and thinking about his grade school years could bring Bert down real fast.

Mike Jackson hustled out the locker room door in his shirtsleeves and said something to Scotty. All Bert heard was the word "Camille." They both hustled back, and Bert followed.

Scotty stood at the little tiled curb that keeps the water from running out of the shower entrance onto the concrete floor. All the showers were going full blast. Bert was standing on his tiptoes beside Jackson looking into the shower area over the tiled wall. Camille sat on the floor in the blast from one of the showers, his chin on his chest.

Bert saw Scotty say something to Camille, but he was too far away to hear through all the shower noise. Scotty picked up two towels from the pile on the table by the entrance and stepped in. He turned off the shower in his path and the one spraying down on Camille. Scotty wiped his face with one of the towels and said something else, but Bert still couldn't hear. Camille said something. Scotty tossed the towel down onto Camille's shoulder. Camille looked up and said something, then he started crying again.

Bert's calves were hurting and he settled back down off his toes.

Scotty leaned forward and extended his arm. Bert didn't have to strain to see because Scotty was so tall. In a second Camille appeared. He put his arms around his father's neck and cried hard. Loud enough for anyone in the locker room to hear.

Bert sat on the north end of the 7-Eleven sidewalk eating slowly the first of what would be a number of hot dogs. The Sportster sat a few feet farther north in the big dirt lot between the 7-Eleven and the yogurt store. The 7-Eleven hadn't become a Thompson hangout at this point. Tonight would be the night that made it one.

Bert was savoring his dog, capturing with his tongue each errant slice of jalapeño pepper and onion chunk that clung to the napkin. Bert was surprised to see Camille's station wagon roll past the gas pumps and into the dirt lot. Public Enemy continued pounding out of the stereo after Shepard shut down. Bert could see the sides and top of the old rig vibrating. Zimster could add hearing loss to his list of handicaps. Shepard and Jackson climbed out slowly. They walked as though various parts of their bodies would have preferred to be home in bed. Bert had assumed Camille wouldn't feel like going out on the town after the incident in the shower. But then Bert didn't really know Camille.

Both boys crawled into the back of the Chevy. They emerged hoisting an old easy chair to which Jim Zimster was secured by a series of bungee cords. They placed the chair on the blacktop a few inches from Bert's Big Gulp cup. Zimster unhooked the cords and took a breath. Everybody spoke a greeting, including Jackson, with whom Bert had never spoken. Shepard adjusted the watch cap he was wearing over his wet head. "We mean to rid this place of some hot dogs," he said.

It made Bert smile. Shepard sounded like his dad. There was just that little accent.

More Thompson kids began pulling in. Lauren Haskell parked her Karmann-Ghia beside Camille's Chevy. Then a bunch of sophomore boys showed up, then Clara Davis and Sharon Jackson, Mike's sister, then Darby and Sean Christman in Darby's Tracker with the top down. All the stereos gave way to Public Enemy.

People gravitated around Zimster's chair. Bert sort of knew these people, but he didn't feel particularly comfortable around any of them, and that included Darby and Camille. He wasn't sure about Zimster. Bert was a little peeved. All he'd wanted to do was eat a peaceful two or three hot dogs.

Bert heard footsteps and looked up to see Krista James. She wore jeans and a sweatshirt that said THOMPSON VOLLEYBALL. Krista always looked good, but she looked particularly good tonight with her cheeks flushed in the cool air. It hurt to look at Krista because she was so beautiful. What hurt was that Bert knew he would never touch this beauty, would never have Krista or any girl like her. Bert also knew that beauty wasn't a quality that needed to be touched to be appreciated, and he knew that human beings didn't exist to be possessed. But this knowledge didn't prevent Krista James's beauty from tearing at Bert's heart.

Bert took a peek over at Darby. The Darb was by no means eclipsed by Krista. Darby had a look and she had a way. She also had a Sean Christman. Lauren Haskell was sleek and cute as an otter and seemed just as playful with Kelly-Mac. And Bert had never noticed until tonight how good-looking Sharon Jackson was. Even his childhood friend Clara Davis was looking good to Bert, and she was big and tough enough to beat him up.

Bert wanted to scream. Goddammit! I came here for a hot dog not a hard-on! But he contained himself.

Camille asked Jim what he wanted on his dog, then he and Mike ambled inside. In less than a minute everybody was inside lined up for dogs or nosing around in the aisles, and Bert and Jim were alone.

Bert wanted to say something, so he asked how Jim knew Camille. Jim said they had European History together. "Can I ask you a favor, Bert?" Jim said.

Bert said sure.

"Tell me if you don't want to," Jim said.

"Come on," Bert said.

"Would you mind getting my chair out of Camille's car and helping me into the bathroom?"

"I wouldn't mind," Bert replied.

As Bert hauled the wheelchair out of the car and set it up he was remembering back to fifth grade when every kid in class but Zimster had been happy to tell Mr. Lawler when Bert was acting like he thought he was more important than anybody else. Every kid but Zimster. They hadn't done it out of meanness, most of them. They were just little kids happy to please their teacher. They didn't know much about being people. But Zimster knew. Bert was grateful to have the chance to repay some of this debt.

Camille and Mike set Jim back in the big chair and Bert returned the wheelchair to the Chevy. It was a lot more pleasant messing around in there with no music going. More pleasant, that is, until Bert realized why there was no music going: Krista James was sitting in the driver's seat looking through the tapes. She looked up in the dim yellow glow of the old dome light. If girls get more beautiful than this, Bert thought, one look at them would stop your heart.

"It was good of you to help Jim," Krista said.

"I've know him since grade school," Bert said.

"I know him from European History," Krista said. "He's smart and he's got a wicked sense of humor."

In that moment Bert was stricken by a thought: What do you do for a love life if you're among the Zimsters of the world? Can you masturbate? Pray to all the powers of the universe that you can. Please let there be a Zimsterland.

Krista was talking to him. She repeated herself. "Any requests, I said."

"Well," Bert replied. "I like ZZ Top."

"You're not going to believe it," Krista said. She waved a tape box.

Bert went in for another dog. He squirted a thick line of melted cheese up both sides, then over the cheese a thicker layer of chili, then over the chili just the thinnest line of mustard. He wrapped the dog in extra napkins to catch the spillage, then heaped on the jalapeño slices and onion chunks. There are some desires that transcend a concern for fresh breath.

Krista was sitting in Bert's place dipping into a giant bag of Cheetos when he returned. She and Shepard, Jim and Mike, Darby and Sean, Lauren and Kelly-Mac, and Clara and Sharon were absorbed in something.

Bert sat on the sidewalk a few feet behind the rest of the kids. He leaned against the store wall. He took a big, messy, luscious bite of dog. This was all right. He would watch and he would listen. It was what he did best.

Krista told Camille she'd heard he was crying in the locker room, and she asked why. Everybody but Krista and Camille—and Bert—looked away in embarrassment.

But Camille wasn't embarrassed. He said he hadn't seen his dad for four years and hadn't been to the States since he was eight. He'd put in all those years dreaming about coming to the States and doing the stuff his dad had done growing up. He was in the shower feeling good about having caught a few balls, and the realization all at once came upon him that he was finally getting to do the things he'd dreamed of for so long.

Sharon asked why Camille didn't get to visit his dad all those years. Her brother glared at her. Bert had the feeling Mike knew Camille's story. She asked if it was because his mother wouldn't let him.

"She wouldn't let me," Camille said. "But it wasn't because she and my dad don't get along. My dad was an agent for the Bureau of Alcohol, Tobacco and Firearms, and he got shot."

Bert sat up straighter. He remembered what Scotty'd said about his knees: *One knee went in football and the other in an accident in my job.*

"I had my plane ticket and was all set to go see him in Tucson," Camille said. "I'd flown by myself before. But then he called and said I'd better not come, that he'd been shot while he was undercover and that they hadn't rounded up all the guys he'd been investigating. My mom about shit.

"That was ten years ago," Camille said, "and she only let me come this year because my uncle Steve convinced her those guys weren't still looking for Dad. Steve's an agent—"

Kelly-Mac interrupted. "The biker who tried to pick a fight with Coach is a cop?" he said.

Bert and Zimster spoke at the same time. "He's really a nice guy," they said.

People laughed at how perfectly synchronized they were.

Well, that explains a few things, Bert thought.

"Steve's with ATF," Camille said. "He's on leave now. He just hates to dress up."

Bert could see that Camille had talked about himself all he wanted to. And he saw that Krista saw it too. She turned to Zimster, held up a Cheeto and asked what he thought it resembled. It didn't resemble anything Bert could think of. Maybe a white radish. Except that it was orange.

Jim blushed. The addition of color to his pasty cheeks looked good, but he was not pleased with the attention. He glared at Jackson and Shepard, then back at Krista. "I didn't make it up," he said. "In spite of what these two probably told you."

"Make what up?" asked Kelly-Mac.

"It's a known fact," Zimster said. "Granted, it's not widely known. But nevertheless it's a fact."

"What is?" Steve Thonski asked.

Krista gobbled down the Cheeto upon which all eyes were focused, dug into the bag for another, then held it up. "According to Jim Zimster," she said, "one bag out of every lot of Cheetos bags produced contains—" Krista interrupted herself. "How many bags in a lot, Jim?"

"A lotta bags in a lot," snarled Pat Sweat through clenched teeth. "A lotta goddamn bags in a lot. Now what are you guys talking about?"

"About ten thousand, I think," Zimster said.

"One out of every ten thousand or so Cheetos bags," Krista continued, "contains an exact replica of a penis."

"Awesome!" shouted Kevin Robideaux. "Radical!" shouted one of his sophomore friends. The whole bunch of them laughed and pummeled one another in typical sophomore fashion as they raced to the door.

"Not an exact replica," Jim said. "It's exactly proportioned, but scaled down. I'm not sure what the ratio is."

"Exact?" said Darby. "How could it be exact? They're all different."

"Since when are you a penis expert, Granger?" Lauren Haskell asked.

"She's got four brothers," Christman said.

The first of the sophomores had returned and was distributing handfuls of Cheetos around the group. People were holding Cheetos at arm's length, tilting their heads, squinting, consulting their neighbors' perspective.

Clara and Sharon got up and went to buy a bag of their own.

It did strike Bert as a clever marketing ploy. He was witnessing the early stages of a Cheeto frenzy at this moment.

"They're so orange," Lauren said. It got more difficult to understand her as the number of Cheetos she was chewing increased. "And they leave a residue." She held her hands palms-out and fingers-wide. "You've really got to scrub to get it off."

Zimster, Jackson, and Shepard howled at this. Bert laughed too. Krista James wore a big smile.

Was it possible to get drunk on Cheetos? Probably not. But it was possible to get silly when you mixed them with ingenuity. And sex.

One of the sophomores spoke through a spray of tiny orange granules. "You don't suppose there's like a miniature . . . you know . . . in every box of Cheerios?"

"Nasty!" Jackson said.

Zimster and Bert joined in the derisive chorus.

Clara and Sharon appeared clutching a big Cheetos bag between them. "These things are good," Sharon said as she plunged her hand in again. "I can't keep 'em outa my mouth." She looked at Clara. Their eyes grew big and their cheeks puffed.

When their laughter burst they sprayed Cheetos chunks all down the backs of the sophomore boys who were on their knees emptying their Cheetos bags onto the blacktop.

Over the laughter and cursing Bert heard the rumble of a Harley-Davidson. Camille's head turned at the same time and they looked at each other.

Around the corner and into the light rode Scotty with Rita on behind. They wore jeans, plain leather jackets, and navy blue watch caps like Camille's. Rita had her hair in a braid. They waved and walked into the store. It was clear that they didn't want to interrupt.

But they were back outside in half a minute and walking over to the group.

"You kids ate this store out of hot dogs," Scotty said.

Rita looked at the scattered Cheetos. "Nothing like hot

dogs and Cheetos to ease the pain of losing a close one," she said. She tucked some loose hair under her watch cap. She's twice as old, Bert thought, but she's as beautiful as Krista.

"We're gone," Scotty said.

"You children have fun," said Rita.

Scotty and Rita had settled onto the bike when Camille got to his feet in an uncharacteristically graceless manner and hobbled over. He said something, kissed Rita on the cheek, then put his arms around his dad and gave him a smooch. He stood there in the bright light from the store windows waving as he watched them turn south on Division and roll away.

When Camille returned to the group Krista got him talking about his dad and Rita, which was easy to do. Everybody listened with interest, particularly Bert Bowden, who knew a good story when he heard one.

Chapter 19

He Hath Borne Me on His Back a Thousand Times

It has not been a good day for Bert. He turned in his Camille Shepard profile and Darby held it in her hand as though she were weighing it, looked at him with sad astonishment, and said, "Bowden, you are such an egg. You are such an incredible, inedible egg. Did *The Explorer* get into book publishing while I was at lunch?"

"I liked it," the Hmongster said. He walked over from the darkroom and tossed a fat file folder on the table. "And we've got mass photos."

"I'll read it when I can," Darb Varder said, "and maybe by spring I'll have cut it down to a length we can use."

The piece was a little long—forty-eight pages. Bert knew he'd gotten carried away. He'd tried to keep it short. But the more he learned about Camille and Scotty and Rita and Steve and Camille's mom and both his grandfathers and even his stepdad, the more fascinated he became. And if it was fascinating to him, why wouldn't it be fascinating to other people? Bert knew he was a little off-center, but he didn't think he was *that* different from everybody else.

Maybe he could break it into separate articles. Like

the stuff about French schools. The French school system was an academic Marine Corps compared to the American system. A contributing cause of Camille's breakdown in the shower was probably delayed stress. Who wouldn't be interested in that?

Bert's problem was that he was interested in everything. That was one of his problems, anyway.

The profile was one thing that went wrong. Then at work Bert put his coffee cup on the stove to keep it warm, and it melted. It was plastic. And it was the second plastic cup he'd done that to.

Steve, who'd walked in the back door, noticed it right away. "What's that ugly shit on the stove?" he said.

It had been a Sinclair gas station cup. Mostly white, red lettering, green handle, green dinosaur. What remained was still mostly white, but that was the only resemblance. It looked like a mutant marshmallow that had melted off the roasting stick. But the green and the little swirl of red added a vomitous quality.

Before Scotty or Dave could expose Bert as the dufus responsible, Steve spoke again. "Don't tell me," he said. "The last two remaining California condors flew in here and took a tandem dump?"

Scotty walked back into the showroom and Dave returned to grinding valves. Bert remained at the computer, where he was logging parts. "No, huh?" Steve said. "Well, I guess Bootsie was keepin' his coffee hot in a plastic cup again?"

Bert rose from his chair, grabbed some welding gloves and a chisel, and scraped the malodorous goo off the stove. "I get all these parts numbers in my head, and I just forget," he said.

On his way out Steve stopped behind Bert's chair. "Make sure you stay off your head goin' home, Bootsie," he said. "It might be about time to put that H-D away for the year." He whacked Bert on the shoulder with his gloves and walked out.

It is about time to put the bike away, Bert thought as he rode home from work. He didn't mind the cold, particularly since he'd started wearing goggles. If you kept your eyes from freezing, late fall weather actually made for pretty nice riding. But now that Thanksgiving had come and gone Bert was doing most of his riding in the dark when the streets were shiny with dew. It was dark going to school and dark coming home from work. The streets were always wet, but Bert didn't have the experience to tell when they were also slick. Sometimes the dew froze, and then just a little throttle brought the back wheel spinning out sideways. And that was scary. So Bert rode more slowly and with greater care. Still, it was neat to be riding at all and he hated to give it up.

Bert was surprised to find both his parents' cars in the garage when the door cranked up. It seemed like his mom was always showing a house, or his dad was at a dinner meeting. When he walked into the kitchen and saw them both he knew his grandfather was dead.

His mom was leaning against the sink looking down at his dad. His dad was sitting at the little table looking at something wrapped in aluminum foil that he held in his hands. He was wearing his overcoat.

The feeling that came to Bert had nothing to do with Gramp. It was about his folks. It was that they were strangers to him. He'd lived all his life with them, he loved them, but he didn't know them.

"Your grandfather's out of his misery," Donald Bowden said. "We just got the call. I was on my way down there with some leftover turkey. I was almost out the door."

The way his dad was hefting the turkey made Bert think of Darby with his story.

"Don't need the turkey now," Bert's dad said as he rose from the table. He tossed the package into the fridge. "But I've got to get down there. And I've got to stop and tell your grandmother."

A glaze covered Bert's dad's face. It was like dew on a dark street. Why is he saying *your grandfather*? Bert wondered. Why doesn't he say *my father*?

Bert's mother caught his eye. The nod of her head and the expression on her face told him what he should do.

"I'll go with you," Bert said.

Bert thought they were headed for Gram's, but his dad drove to the home first. He made the arrangements with the night supervisor while Bert waited in the hall. I'll never walk to Gramp's room again, Bert thought. Never in all my life. He wanted to walk there one more time.

The little plastic nameplate with ALBERT BOWDEN was still on the door. Bert pulled it off and put it in his jacket pocket. He would give it to his dad. He turned on the light and looked at Gramp's bed. He knew the body was there, he'd heard the supervisor say it was. There was just so little left of Gramp that it hardly made a bump.

Bert wanted to see Gramp again. He knew Gramp was gone, that this was only his body. But this body had been Gramp for all Bert's life, and he wanted to see it one more time.

He pulled down the sheet and looked. The sight filled Bert with reverence, dread, and wonder simultaneously and in equal proportions. The man was a mummy. He was shrunken and withered and looked like he'd been dead for a long time. Bert had seen his grandfather five days before and, except for the rise and fall of his chest, Bert thought he'd looked dead then. But he hadn't looked like this.

With his eyes Bert saw the husk of his grandfather. But in his mind he saw Gramp at his most vibrant. It was this difference between the Gramp that was dead here in front of his eyes and the Gramp that lived in his memory that awed Bert so.

Bert thought of Shakespeare's *Hamlet*. It was the look of his grandfather's head, so like a skull, that caused him to think of the play his class had read last year.

Hamlet and his friend Horatio are walking in the cemetery and one of the gravediggers spades up a skull. He tells Hamlet it belonged to Yorick, a court jester. It was Hamlet's father's court that Yorick had been jester in. Hamlet turns to his friend and says the famous lines, "Alas! poor Yorick. I knew him, Horatio: a fellow of infinite jest, of most excellent fancy: he hath borne me on his back a thousand times. . . ." Bert remembered the lines because everyone in class had had to memorize a famous speech, and he had chosen this one.

Bert believed he had an intellectual understanding of the passage then, but now he understood it with his heart.

How many times and in how many different ways did Gramp carry me on his back? Bert thought. And he's carrying me right now, even though he's gone from this world. I feel his love lifting me up.

Bert reached to touch his grandfather's face one last time. As he did he heard his father's voice. "Jesus Christ, Bert!"

Donald Bowden stepped forward and whipped the sheet back over his father's body. Then he turned and looked down at his son. "What is wrong with you?" he said.

Bert didn't know how to reply.

Bert's uncle Doug was there when they arrived at Gram's. He put his arm around Bert and gave him a sad smile. He didn't say anything, but the way he tilted his head and raised his eyebrows said, We knew it was coming, but it's still tough to believe.

Bert hugged his grandmother. "I'm sorry, Gram," he whispered.

"Berty," she said as she patted his back, "I prayed and prayed for this. Your grandfather is better off where he is now. Don't you be sad."

"Bert can stay with you tonight, Mom," Donald Bowden said. "If you need anything he can get it, or you can call me."

Bert kept one arm around Gram's shoulder as he turned to look at his dad. He was happy to stay, he just hadn't known that was the plan.

Bert tried to read the emotion in his father's face. It seemed closer to perplexity than sadness. Bert had seen this expression before. This was how his dad looked when he had a problem at work. He wasn't sad; he was pissed off. His words at the home rang in Bert's ears: *Jesus Christ, Bert! What is wrong with you?*

Bert squeezed Gram's shoulders a little tighter. "I always want to stay with my gram," he said.

Bert's father left then. Doug stayed to watch the late news and to eat some soft-boiled eggs and toast. Then he hugged his mother and gave her a kiss on the cheek. Bert watched them at the door.

Gram was in the bathroom washing her face. She had left the door open, and Bert could see her reflection in the mirror on the door. He was pulling out the sofa bed. The TV was off. "Gram," he said, "do you think Doug takes after Gramp more, or does my dad?"

Bert saw her bend to the sink. He heard her splash the water. She didn't reply for a while. "Children don't always take after their parents," she said. She walked into the living room drying her face with a towel. Bert could smell her scented soap. "Douglas is more like his father than Donald. But you're more like your grandfather than either of his sons."

Edith Bowden wore a long flannel nightgown. White with tiny red roses. She snugged her hairnet over her head. "I guess the scientists have it about figured out now," she said. "They know what gene does what. They could make a baby that would grow into whatever kind of person they wanted. I raised your father and your uncle and your aunt. Those children grew up in the same house with the same parents, they ate the same food, went to the same school. And each one is different from the others. And they're all so different from your grandfather and me that no one would even guess we were related. It's a mystery to me, Berty."

She kissed Bert on the cheek and told him good night. She closed her door, but then she opened it right away. She told Bert he could watch TV if he wanted, that it wouldn't bother her. Then she wished him sweet dreams.

Bert lay in the dark on his grandmother's sofa and considered his grandfather's absence from the world. Gramp hadn't been Gramp for a long time. But now he was nothing. He wasn't in the world anymore. Maybe he was somewhere. He was in Bert's memory for sure and forever. But he was not in the world. It didn't make Bert sad exactly. It was more amazing than sad. Bert had loved this man.

Bert had kissed him on the lips, received his whisker burns, they had smoked his pipe together. How could he disappear from the world? And yet he had.

Bert stayed with Gram the next day. He asked if he could rearrange Gramp's workshop a little, and she said okay. The first thing he did was to make a fire in the stove, then bring out her old coffeepot, make some coffee, and keep his cup—a ceramic cup—warm on the stovetop. He moved boards and tools into the garage. He vacuumed and then he washed the floor and walls with hot, soapy water. From the rafters of the garage he brought down Gramp's old army-surplus cot and set it up in one corner. He slept on it that night. The next day he went home at lunch and packed the stuff he needed from his room. He slept warmer that night under his comforter.

The following day, after Gramp's funeral, Bert asked his mom if she minded him staying at Gram's for a while. She said Gram didn't have room, and Bert replied that he'd fixed up the workshop a little.

Jean Bowden looked at her son as though he were someone she'd known a long time ago, someone for whom she'd had great affection but could no longer quite recognize. "Of course you can, Bert," she said. "Of course you can stay with your grandmother."

Chapter 20

Not a Harley Guy

If it hadn't been such a beautiful morning, Bert might not have parted with the Sportster. It had been cold and clear and still, an appropriate setting in which to part from delusion. Bert had known for a long time he wasn't a Harley guy. He wished he were the kind of guy who fit on such a machine—a guy like Camille Shepard— but he wasn't and he never would be. Bert didn't believe he was nothing, as his father thought. He wasn't much, but he wasn't nothing. He was honest. He knew what he was, and he was honest enough not to lie to himself about it.

But maybe it hadn't been the beauty of the morning that made him do it. Maybe it had been the night before when Camille caught eleven passes and scored three TDs to lead Thompson's 27–26 thumping of Gonzaga Prep, undefeated and ranked first in the state until this final game of the season. Maybe Bert just couldn't stand that he wasn't a guy like Camille Shepard and so he couldn't stand owning and riding around on a machine that showed the world so conspicuously he wished he were. Camille had had Coach Heslin cut off his ponytail with a pair of tape scissors in the second quarter because he couldn't get the refs to keep number 22 on the defense from pulling it. Bert's imagination could not compete with such real-world studliness.

"You don't have to be tough to be a Harley guy, Bert," Scotty said after work. "You don't have to pretend to be tough. You just have to like riding a Harley.

"Maybe you're a Triumph guy," he said. "Or a BSA guy. I wouldn't be surprised if you turned out to be a Norton guy. We'll get as many dollars as we can out of the Sportster, then we'll keep our eyes peeled for a new ride for you."

Bert brought sweats with him so he could run home, and he was bundled up good when he walked out of the bathroom to where Scotty and Dave were sitting by the stove. Rita had arrived while Bert was dressing. Scotty's workout bag sat by his chair. The racquetball gloves fastened around the straps always made Bert think of the pelts of little animals. Scotty and Rita were headed for a workout.

Scotty had been after Bert to try playing racquetball. He said it was a great sport for gimpy old farts like him and solitary guys like Bert. Rita directed the aerobics program at the club where Scotty played. She said Bert would like it there. Bert told them he was thinking about it. And he was.

His sweats were soaked by the time he chugged through Gram's gate. He ate in the wet clothes, then walked out to his room, popped in a tape, built a fire, and sat down at the keyboard to cut the Camille Shepard profile. Through his headset Bert listened to his standard inspirational tunes by Bob Seger, Bruce Springsteen, Eric Clapton, George

Thorogood, ZZ Top, The Fabulous Thunderbirds, and the Jeff Healey Band, along with tunes by Bob Dylan and Bonnie Raitt whose music Scotty had introduced him to. Listening to rock and roll *was* like riding a motorcycle. It vibrated through you that same way, and it shut out the world—all the parts of the world you didn't want to let in.

Bert listened to tunes and cut the article until he had it down to eight pages.

Darby printed it without changing a word.

Chapter 21

The Second Best Thing

Tanneran has told Bert he can be a writer. Bert wants to be somebody, and writing might be a way to do it. He loves to read, and he likes to write, but he's never thought about *being* a writer. The idea of creating for others the pleasure he finds in books is appealing, all right. But it's also incomprehensible. What does Bert Bowden know that someone else would want to hear? And yet, because a man he trusts says he can do it, and because he so badly wants to do *something*, Bert entertains the notion.

Bert's greatest dream and secret desire is to be an athlete. But Bert is not a stupid guy. The world has shown him that this isn't going to happen. So what can he do? He can do the second best thing.

Bert withdraws his last essay from his folder and reads Tanneran's note for the zillionth time:

Bert, I was so engaged by "Peckered" that half the songs on my Dylan *Slow Train Comin'* tape played through while I was reading and I didn't hear a word or a note. I love that tape, so your making me deaf to it is high praise.

You're a funny guy, Bert. Smart and funny. These qualities come through in your prose. In class, however, you're one of the living dead, and I want you to come alive.

You have a style. A developed style is unusual for a sixteen-year-old kid, and this is what I want to talk to you about.

I think you can be a writer, Bert.

What do I mean by *writer*? What I mean is a professional story writer—somebody who sees so deeply and clearly into human life and then writes with such precision, insight, compassion, and imagination about it that the world gives him or her a reward. The reward might not be money; it might be respect. But because there is value, there is also reward.

I know: You're thinking that you're just a kid. True. But consider this: S. E. Hinton wrote *The Outsiders* when she was sixteen; Françoise Sagan wrote *Bonjour Tristesse* when she was eighteen, and Stephen King was writing when he was in high school and sold his first stories when he was in college.

Better yet, consider this: You know kids playing
sports at Thompson who in five years, with any
luck at all, will be playing professionally. They will
be rewarded for doing a thing they love. It's true
that all the writers in the world who make as much
as pro athletes could get together in the teachers'
lunchroom and there'd still be chairs left for the
entire Thompson band. But money isn't the point.
The point is doing the thing you love to do. And
for a writer the point is also having the honor of
taking part in a tradition that's as old as human life
on earth. Back when people wore animal hides the
tribal storytellers were honored with the place
closest to the fire. Now they get the place closest
to Oprah Winfrey.

That's a joke. It's after one A.M. You keep me up
late, Bert, and you make me forget that Dylan's on
the box. You must be a good writer!

The reason I bring up the kids with chances to
become professional athletes isn't that they're
models for making lots of dough. It's because
they're models for starting early to be what they
want to be. These kids—and also some actors,
musicians, dancers, graphic artists, and auto
mechanics—are preparing right now for the thing

they want to make happen in five years. They're
starting to make it happen now.

If you want to be a writer, Bert, you can start now.

I'm not suggesting you sign a blood oath in your
diary or make a pilgrimage to the Hemingway gun
collection down in Ketcham or take up smoking
and drinking too much coffee or wearing a cape or
any other crazed artsy-fartsy shit.

Being good at anything is real hard, and if we
want to be good at something as complex and
comprehensive as writing stories we need to
realize it's going to take a long time, and we've
got to get in gear.

You might think you need a "gift" to be a writer,
Bert. Well, don't think so, because it isn't true.
Writing, like most difficult things in life, takes
more guts than brains. It takes "desire"—you've
got to want to do it—and then out of your desire
comes "tenacity," the ability to hold on.

The greatest gift a person can have is desire, Bert,
and I know you have it. If you want to focus your
desire on writing, let's get together and outline a
course of action.

Tanneran

Tanneran was right—Bert knew it. He had desire. That was something Lawler hadn't taken from him. Bert also knew, however, that so far in his life his desire hadn't brought about any achievement.

Tanneran's advice was that Bert spend his time and energy learning about writing so that when a story called to him from his life and when he was sure he wanted to answer it and sit down for all those hours, he'd have the skills to write it. You develop those skills, Tanneran said, from line-by-line reading of the best writing you can find, then trying to write your own stories like the masters.

Tanneran told Bert to be thankful for the pain in his life, not resentful, because out of that pain would come knowledge. He told Bert that most important of all was to be patient, because it would be a long haul.

He gave Bert a list of books: *Love Medicine* by Louise Erdrich, *The Things They Carried* by Tim O'Brien, *A Childhood: The Biography of a Place* by Harry Crews, and *The World According to Garp* by John Irving. The only one Bert had heard of was *Garp* because he'd seen the movie. Tanneran said to read through them once for the story, then to study them.

Bert is beginning the study phase tonight. He's starting with *Love Medicine*. It was the first one he read, but some of the stuff in it stayed with him even while he was reading the others, which were also great. His goal is to discover how Erdrich captured him away from the real world and brought him into her imagined one.

Bert's favorite characters are Lipsha Morrisey and Howard Kashpaw, who is also called King Junior. Lipsha is sort of lost until he discovers who his father is. He and his dad only get to spend a little time together, but they like each other, and Bert could tell that's what turns Lipsha around.

Howard Kashpaw is a younger kid whose dad, King, is a massive asshole. Howard has always thought of himself as King Junior until one day at school his teacher is calling roll and she reads off his whole name, King Howard Kashpaw Junior, and asks which of these names he'd like to be called. He never realized he had a choice. He chooses Howard. Then another day the class is cutting out paper hearts for Valentine's Day. They write their names in the heart with black Magic Marker. When Howard sees his heart up on the board with his name on it he has a kind of spiritual experience. Bert wrote the word "epiphany" in the margin. He learned it in Tanneran's class. It means *a sudden manifestation of the essence or meaning of something*. What is manifest to Howard is the knowledge that he's himself and not his dad. And this knowledge sets him free to be himself.

Bert wishes Louise Erdrich would write another book about Howard so he could find out if he maintains that independence as he gets older. Even if your dad's an asshole, it's awful tough to keep from wanting him to like you.

Chapter 22

Bert Joins the Club

Bert pedals hard on the stationary bike. The music blasting up from the aerobics room vibrates through the walls, the floor, the bike, the air, and into Bert. The sensation is like riding a motorcycle. The beat of the music pulses like pistons, and the sexual effluvium emanates from the aerobicizing bodies like oil burning on a hot engine. An erotic quality fills the air and clings like a preorgasmic secretion.

Bert has tried aerobics. He has been down on the floor among those bodies. But he can't endure it. Neither can he turn away completely. So he rides the stationary bike at the railing above the aerobics room, loses himself in music and fantasy, and pretends not to look down.

Some of the women wear tight black sports bras and nothing else over their knee-length shorts. Even harder to endure than the black bras over naked belly buttons, though, is another kind of leotard some of them wear. These cover more of their upper bodies, but they taper down to a tiny string of fabric that runs between the women's legs and bisects their butts into pairs of hard, sweet, dancing, neon ham-buns.

It's those tiny strings that did Bert in. They focused his

attention, then they wrapped around it and squeezed. And he could not endure the beauty and the sensuality. Bert wanted to be one of those strings of fabric rubbed to a musky tatter in that dark swamp of swirling stars.

Bert's enthusiasm for the club is running out at the same pace as the two-week membership Scotty and Rita gave him for Christmas. His stomach is sore from the abdominal machine, his thighs and butt are sore from the StairMaster, his powers of fantasy are travel-weary from so many trips to Bowdenland with various of the aerobics women and all of the aerobics girls. And the thin ego he brought to the club has been pounded flat as the red lines on the racquet-ball courts by everyone he played with.

Bert has been demolished by a woman his mother's age, a man older than his grandmother who is right-handed but played lefty, a fat college girl, and a junior-high boy.

In spite of not being good at the game, however, Bert gets a feeling of satisfaction out of hitting that little blue ball. He just wishes he could hit the goddamned thing where he wants to.

Bert's dad will give him a membership to the club if he wants one. What Berts wants is to fit in at the club. But membership doesn't assure that. Nothing assures that. Bert knows that fitting in takes time, particularly in a setting where physical beauty, power, and skill are the dues for true membership. He knows he doesn't have what it takes to pay in that currency. And he knows that neither his father nor anyone else can give it to him.

Bert's mom has offered to buy him some workout clothes, but he's asked her to wait till he decides if he's going to join. The truth is that Bert would love some new clothes for the club, but he'd be embarrassed to wear them. What he would love even more, however— and what neither his mother nor anyone else can give him—is the body to wear that stuff. He likes the bright colors, particularly in the tank tops. But if a guy's going to expose that much flesh, it should be toned flesh, and Bert's flesh is not toned. Bert's flesh makes him think of pasta. He's a five-foot-nine-inch chunk of Bertolini cooked too long.

Bert's legs are okay. He might be able to get by in a pair of the skintight, knee-length shorts that both guys and girls wear. But he really can't see himself styled out like that. The image just won't form itself in his head.

The bike beeps to signal Bert that his twenty minutes are up. He keeps his eyes closed as he climbs off, and he doesn't open them until he has turned and can no longer see through the railing down into the aerobics room. He looks down into the racquetball courts and sees they're all filled. He won't be practicing racquetball this evening.

After Bert showers he stops at the desk to drop his towel in the bag and pick up his keys. On the counter he sees that the sign-up sheets for winter racquetball leagues are out. They can't have been out long because there's only one name. Bert bends to the B sheet.

For a second the sound is turned off in Bert's head.

There is only the pulsing clarity of this name printed in blue ink: GARY LAWLER.

Bert walks back through the glass doors into the work-out area and the sound comes on in his head again. There are many sounds here: the thin swoosh of the stationary bike pedals, the clank of the plates in the weight machines, the whir of the chains that drive the StairMasters, the aluminum whisper of the seats sliding back and forth on the rowing machines, the music rising up from the aerobics classes.

But Bert doesn't hear these sounds. What Bert hears are the sounds created when racquets make contact with racquet balls, and then the subsequent sounds of those little blue balls contacting walls. He walks along the rail looking down into each court. And then he sees a short, dark guy hitting by himself. That's him, all right. Gary Lawler, Bert's old teacher. He hasn't changed. He looks in great shape. The asshole sonofabitch.

Chapter 23

Bert Bashes His Head

Scotty returned from the classic bike show in Phoenix just in time to scratch Bert's name off the B league list and write him in on C. This saved Bert the embarrassment of playing men and women against whom he might not have scored a single point, and it saved those B players the wasted time of playing someone who wasn't experienced enough to give them a game.

Scotty's first thought had been to put Bert in with the novices where he belonged. But he figured the kid would ask for help and that he'd have him playing good C racquetball after a couple sessions on the court, so C is where he put him. He told Bert what he'd done the next evening in the locker room when he saw him ripping the clear plastic off the handle of a two-hundred-dollar racquet.

Bert looked up, and for the first time Scotty saw in his face the boy Donald Bowden might have been referring to when he said *a kid like Bert*. "I knew you wouldn't have any fun in B," Scotty said.

"Thanks," Bert replied. "I guess I got carried away."

"I think C'll be plenty of challenge for you," Scotty said.

Bert handed Scotty the racquet he'd borrowed. "Thanks very much for lending me this," he said.

League racquetball started the first week in January, and it didn't take many matches for Bert to realize Scotty had been right. Bert wouldn't have had any fun in B. He wasn't having any fun in C. He would have to score no points at all to get beat worse than he was getting beat by the C players. It was humiliating.

Bert had bought a used copy of *Strategic Racquetball* by Steve Strandemo and Bill Bruns when he signed up to play league. The explanations were clear, and Bert read the book with care every night. He believed he'd learned a lot about the game in these few weeks. Every time he got out on the court, however, he demonstrated to himself that he couldn't play for shit. It was so humiliating.

Humiliation was the subject of Bert's thoughts as he pressed his forehead to the windows of Thompson's third-floor hall. Winter morning sunlight flowed through the windows in a warm current that bathed his bare arms and his face, but the glass was cold where his forehead touched it. He pressed his palms to the glass, closed his eyes, and side-stepped along the windows, his yellow hall pass fluttering between his fingers. He looked like someone out on a window ledge of a tall building, trying to find a way back inside before he lost his balance.

Bert had more than his share of things to be thankful for, and most of the time he recognized this. Right now, however, he was too frustrated with his life to see it. As he navigated the hallway in this unusual fashion Bert was thankful for three things only: He was thankful for the icy glass against his skin; he was thankful that the hallway was deserted; and he was profoundly thankful that he'd told no one about his futile commitment to get good enough at racquetball to stomp Gary Lawler, to send him home crying, to shove the desk of his soul across the floor of his life into a dark corner and nail it down forever.

It felt good to let out his hatred for Lawler after all these years. It was like breathing again after having held his breath since fifth grade.

It made Bert feel lousy to know he'd probably never get good enough to be in Lawler's league as a racquetball player, let alone beat the guy. But being able to hate the fucker felt sweet. Like the pane of ice against his skin on the tropical third floor of Thompson High.

The fingers of Bert's right hand touched the aluminum molding that framed the glass, then the brick wall. His trip along the windows had ended. He rubbed his left hand over the glass and his right over the bricks of the wall. The tactile distinctions brought a smile to his face. He stepped away from the wall and opened his eyes. Bert had asked for a pass to go to the bathroom, but he didn't need to go to the bathroom. He just needed to get out of Social Problems for a few minutes. Now he would go back.

Bert warmed up on the left side of the court, the backhand side for right-handers like him. Bert wasn't hitting backhands though. He was hitting forehands so he could watch his opponent, who was warming up on the right side.

They'd introduced themselves when they entered the court, but Bert had already forgotten the man's name. He hit neither smoothly nor hard. He hit worse than Bert. He was three times Bert's age, uncoordinated, fat, and slow.

Bert turned and hit a backhand into the floor, then another and another. He wasn't watching the racquet meet the ball. What Bert was doing was saying to himself, I can beat this guy. I can win my first match.

Bert was thinking how friendly his opponent was and hoping that losing wouldn't make him feel too bad when the man's first serve arced off the wall. It hit on the receiving line and bounced high into the side wall above Bert's head. Bert swung his backhand, but all he hit was wall.

"One serves zero," his opponent said.

He hit three more excellent lob serves, and Bert couldn't get a decent return on any of them. One made it to the front wall, but the guy was right there to kill it. Like a fat, hungry bird after a little blueberry.

"Four serving zero."

Bert told himself to settle down. He made sure he was positioned correctly: middle of the court, three feet from the back wall, legs bent. Bert knew that if he could just keep the ball in play, he could beat this guy.

But the serve was perfect. High, slow, bouncing at the receiving line, then high into the back corner. Bert was there, poised, patient. But the ball dropped so tight into the corner that it was unhittable. At least for Bert Bowden. He didn't even swing.

"Five serves zero."

How the fuck are we supposed to play racquetball if I don't get to hit the serve? Bert said to himself. He considered serves this accurate as a form of cheating. He was concentrating on how small he felt for thinking this as the ball bounced by him. He turned and watched it die in the corner.

"Sorry," his opponent said. "You weren't ready."

"No," Bert said. "I was. I mean I wasn't, but I should have been. Your point."

"Six serving zero."

Bert got his strings on this serve and took it to the ceiling. But he hit it too hard. It bounced high off the front wall, then high off the back. It was a bad shot, but it hugged the side wall. The fat guy followed it down the wall, his backhand poised. Bert turned to the front wall and waited for the return. But he didn't hear a hit. He looked back.

"Whiffed it," the fat guy said. He was smiling as he

rubbed his arm. "About pulled my shoulder out of the socket."

I wish, Bert thought.

Bert didn't announce the score. He didn't want it to ring out in the court. He did look back to see that the guy was ready to receive, though. Then he hit a hard drive. It came off low and bounced a couple of inches behind the short line. It bounced again before the guy could take a step.

"Ace!" the guy said. "Great serve."

"One serving six," was Bert's response.

Bert had aces on his mind as he dropped the ball and stepped into it. He hit it solidly, but too low on the wall. It shot past him, and he thought he saw it bounce before the line.

"Short!" the guy said. He caught the ball and flipped it to Bert. "Looked short to me," he said. "Take two if you think it was good."

"No," Bert said. "It was short." These guys are all such good sports, he thought. It made him want to barf. Every person Bert had played since he joined the club acted as though sportsmanship were part of the game. They'd tell him good shot even if it was lucky, they'd play the rally over if one player even came close to hindering the other, and if they hit him with the ball, they'd apologize even if it had been his fault for standing in the way. Such graceful behavior under the pressure of competition didn't come easy to Bert. "Second serve," he announced.

Bert didn't have enough confidence in the accuracy of his hard drive to use it as a second serve, so he hit a lob. Bert's lob was lousy, but he could usually drop it over the short line. Which he did.

The fat guy returned a cripple, and Bert tapped it into the corner.

"Two serves six."

Bert got his first serve in this time. The fat guy returned a bad ceiling shot. Bert returned a bad ceiling shot. The fat guy returned it high off the front wall. Bert let it bounce off the back wall and returned it high off the front. That little blue ball ricocheted around the court in an orthography that said *Out of control!* Not one shot hit the front wall lower than five feet from the floor.

The fat guy hit another blast that bounced off the back wall and carried nearly to the front again. Bert hustled after it and tapped it into the corner.

"Great rally," the fat guy gasped from the backcourt, where he stood panting and dripping sweat onto the floor. He shook his head. "Great hustle. You get to everything."

"Thanks," Bert said.

Bert took three more points and tied it. He served no aces, hit no good shots of any kind. He was able to keep the ball in play and put away the cripples, however, and his opponent wasn't.

The guy kept serving that good lob, and Bert kept hitting bad returns when he was able to return it at all. He knew that if he could just keep the ball in play he'd run the guy into cardiac arrest. But the racquet handle kept turning in his hand. Even with a dry glove he couldn't get a decent grip. He lost the first game 15–9.

Bert served first in game two and double-faulted. He couldn't keep the racquet from turning in his hand. He was down 6–zip before he got his head into the game. He was thinking how much he admired this guy for the grace he showed in competition, and he wondered how people develop such self-control.

Bert broke service only four times in game two. When he did win the serve he faulted on every drive, and his lobs floated into backcourt like masochistic balloons. *Give me a nice whack, please*, they said. *Am I in good enough position? Not too high for you? Not too low? Oooh! Ouch! Those strings are so taut. Pound me into a little blue waffle.* And, even though he was a poor player, Bert's opponent did pound them.

It was game-point serving three as Bert watched the ball arc toward him. When it bounced within centimeters of the receiving line and rose high into the side wall yet again, he turned for the door. "Fuck this," he said. He was on his way to the drinking fountain when the ball died in the corner.

"My lob's got eyes today," the fat guy said after Bert banged the court door closed. A self-deprecating smile accompanied his self-deprecating tone.

"Your serve," Bert said.

Bert lunged and leaped and swatted at the serves and got a few back to the wall. He stormed into forecourt and dove for balls the fat guy would try to pinch into the corners. When the guy went to the ceiling, Bert dashed back and took it off the wall, then he'd scramble into forecourt again. He was literally all over the court, on his stomach as often as on his feet. He was only down 7–4 when the fat guy called time to wipe the sweat out of his eyes.

Bert was walking in circles at midcourt, letting his racquet dangle from the safety cord around his wrist, when he looked up and saw Scott Shepard at the railing.

"Jerry's got that lob serve wired," Scotty said. "But you're makin' him work for everything else."

Bert gave a feeble smile and shrugged his shoulders. He lowered his head. The feeling was like a flock of waterfowl winging up through his chest from off the gastric lake of his stomach. He felt the pressure of their wings against his throat. He thought he might throw up. He wondered how long Scotty had been watching. Bert would rather lose every game in his life 15–0 than have Scott Shepard see what a worthless player he is.

Jerry walked into the court and offered Bert his towel. Bert took off his safety glasses and dried his face, then he dried the glasses.

"You look a little pale, Jer," Scotty said. "Want me to call 911?"

Jerry raised his head and smiled. "Kid's rendering me down" was his reply.

Bert called Jerry by name when he thanked him for the use of his towel. He walked to the door, tossed the towel onto Jerry's workout bag, snugged the door shut, and took position to receive service.

Scotty leaned into the corner where the railing meets the wall separating the courts. He smiled and shook his head as Jerry's lob bounced off the receiving line and crawled down the side wall where Bert was not able to peel it off.

8–4.

One of the great things about this sport, Scotty was reminded again, is that you don't have to be an athlete to play it. Whack the ball, chase after it, whack it again. Hard to beat that for a good time. Jerry was nearly fifty years old and more than fifty pounds overweight, and here he was playing a kid a third his age and having the time of his life. And he'd win too—provided he didn't die.

Bert Bowden was not having the time of his life down there. He returned a couple serves, but his shots were wild. Everything was bouncing right back to Jerry's forehand, and Jerry was putting it away.

Scotty could see the boy's misdirected energy boiling off and leaving him brittle with frustration. Bert was try-ing hard, but he wasn't trying hard at the right things. He was quick and his hand–eye coordination was good. He just needed to learn the game. And he needed to loosen up and have some fun down there. The poor kid was tight as a clutch spring.

The score was 12–5 when Scotty had seen enough. He felt bad for Bert, but he was also proud of him. The kid had played shitty and got murdered, but he'd kept his temper. Sometimes there was nothing tougher for a guy to do. This was a compliment Scotty could pay the boy.

The score was 12–5 when Bert told himself he would hit no more backhands. He didn't care where the ball was, he would not hit another backhand. He'd take it to the back wall with his forehand and hope it carried to the front. The book called this a desperation shot, and Bert was desperate.

Bert was more than desperate. All that was keeping him from unraveling was this desire that Scotty not see it happen.

Bert watched the serve arc toward him. It was perfect, of course, like every other shot this fat asshole had made the whole match. Well, maybe it wasn't quite perfect. It bounced off the side wall harder than usual, and there was room to swing. And Bert swung with all his might. A forehand that rocketed the ball into the back wall from less than three feet away, and right back into his face.

Jerry moved faster getting to Bert than he'd moved all match. Bert stood in the corner with his head down, his safety glasses in his gloved hand, rubbing the bridge of his nose with the other. "Where'd it get you?" Jerry asked.

"My glasses caught most of it," Bert said. "I'm all right." He looked down at the ball. It was a perfect light blue. The blue of the oceans as they were painted on the globes in each classroom of the Susan B. Anthony Elementary School a long time ago. A dust bunny, like a wisp of cloud, clung to it where North America would have been if it had been the earth and Bert had been looking down from space. He picked up the blue ball and handed it to Jerry. "Your point," he said.

Bert looked up at the railing, but Scotty wasn't there. He breathed deep, put his glasses back on, and positioned himself to receive service.

"Thirteen serving five."

Bert let the serve bounce twice, caught it, and flipped it to Jerry. Why even try? He couldn't hit the fucking thing. He did the same with the last serve. "Thanks for the game," he said.

Bert left the court without shaking hands. He closed the door with Jerry still inside. It was a busy time at the club, but Bert was alone at this moment. He walked to the doorway that led to the locker rooms and swung his racquet against the metal edge of the door frame. The racquet cracked, but didn't break. Bert hit it twice more until it collapsed into the shape of the number 3. He looked at the twisted strand of Kevlar wrapped in the web of nylon. This amalgamation of synthetics had cost two hundred dollars of the money he'd received from the Sportster.

Bert threw the wreckage to the floor. But he'd forgotten that the safety cord was still looped around his wrist. The shattered frame hit him just above the knee and opened the skin. He ripped the cord from his wrist and his glove flew off with it. He threw again.

What remained of Bert's racquet bounced high, and Scott Shepard caught it as he walked out of the locker room. Scotty was standing at the doorway, close enough for the blood to spatter across his TEAM EKTELON shirt, when Bert gripped the door frame with both hands and brought his head down against the edge.

Scotty dropped the racquet, took two handfuls of Bert's blue sweat-soaked Lacoste shirt, lifted him into the air, and plastered him against the wall.

Blood flowed down the front of Bert's head, and a knob began to rise on the back. The sound of his head meeting the wall was what captured his attention. It resonated, like the sounds inside a racquetball court. Bert felt no pain. Not yet. The pain from the front and the pain from the back met above his ears and dulled each other. Scotty's face was so close it was all Bert could see.

Scotty spoke only loud enough for Bert to hear. "You've got a decision to make," he said. "You need to find a way to earn your own respect, Bert, and you need to find it fast."

Scotty held Bert against the wall. They were eye to eye. Blood covered one side of Bert's face now and had begun dripping off his chin onto Scotty's arms. This is what the aerobics women saw as they came walking down the corridor, their voices and laughter bright as their outfits, their steps as light as if they'd been on their way to class instead of to the showers. They froze. It was as though they were seeing an accident they weren't sure had run its course.

Then Rita pushed through. "Scott!" she said. She clamped both her hands around Scotty's wrist. "Scott," she said up at him. "Scott."

Scotty let Bert slide down the wall until his shoes met the carpet. He turned to Rita. "It's a head cut," Scotty said. "Not much damage, lot of blood."

Scotty put his arm around Bert's shoulders and pulled him close. Bert's blue shirt was purple with blood now. Rita let go of Scotty's wrist. Scotty asked her if she'd run upstairs and get some tape and gauze and a scissors. Rita nodded. She smiled and touched Bert's forehead on the unbloody side. When the women saw Rita's posture relax they relaxed as well and filed through the doorway to their locker room.

"Let's sit right down here on the floor, Bert," Scotty said. "I've got something else to say."

They both leaned against the wall and let themselves slide down. The back of Bert's shirt left a shiny track. They sat on the floor near the door to court one as bodybuilders, aerobics people, and racquetball players walked past. Everybody looked down at the bloody kid. Neither Scotty nor Bert looked up.

"Bert," Scotty said not much louder than he'd spoken before, "if you need some help you've got to ask for it. If you want help with racquetball, I'll help you. And so will ninety-eight percent of the men and women who play here. Racquetball, whatever," he said.

"Go shower up now," Scotty said, "then I'll look at the cut. When you're home tonight I want you to think of the one thing in the world you'd respect yourself most for being able to do, and then I want you to decide what the first step is on the way to doing it."

Bert nodded his head. All he could think of now was that he couldn't stand his life.

Scotty bent forward on his hands and knees, then raised his hips and pushed himself up with his arms. The metal rods in his old-fashioned knee braces strained against the leather and made it squeak. He reached for Bert's hand and pulled him up. Rita arrived with the first-aid stuff as Scotty gave Bert a light shove toward the showers.

Scotty was waiting by the sinks. He sat on the counter and examined Bert's head under the fluorescent lights above the mirror. Bert had a towel around his waist, but it came untucked and slipped to the floor. Scotty was holding his head, so Bert didn't stoop to reach the towel. He was naked and about as close to Scotty as one person can get to another. He thought he should feel self-conscious, but he didn't.

Scotty pinched the skin closed with the fingers of one hand while he taped three thin strips across the cut. Then he taped a gauze pad over it. "That ought to keep you from bleeding to death until you get stitched," he said. "It's my opinion, Bert, that you could use a scar."

Bert stood at the foot of his cot and looked into the little mirror on the wall. Eight black stitches laced the right side of his forehead from a little below his hairline down toward the middle of his eyebrow. He would have a scar, all right.

A quarter inch of thread stuck out of the lowest stitch like a mutant hair. Bert touched it with the tip of his index finger. It was thick and coarse and hard. It made him think of the scene in *The Fly* where Geena Davis discovers the insect hairs on Jeff Goldblum's back.

Bert lay in the dark and listened to the fire pop in the stove. He thought of what Scotty had told him. Bert didn't need to ruminate for even a second about the thing in the world he would most respect himself for being able to do. The answer lay on the surface of his thoughts like crude oil on an Alaska beach. Bert wanted to beat that sonofabitch Gary Lawler at racquetball.

It wasn't much of an ambition, but it was the truth. Bert liked writing, and maybe he'd write something when he got old. But what he'd wanted his whole conscious

life was to be a good athlete, and it would take a good
athlete to beat Lawler.

And what was the first step down this path? It was
getting some help. It was finding someone who knew the
way. It was asking Scott Shepard to coach him.

Chapter 24

It Ain't Magic

Bert's first racquetball lesson took place on the old couch in the back of the shop at Shepard's Classic and Custom after a workday so busy nobody had time to eat. Saturdays were always busy but Saturdays in winter were really crazy because of the number of bikers who rebuilt while the days were short, the nights long, and the weather hostile. As Bert wrote up orders for Superblend main bearings, low-compression pistons and Stellite valves, swing-arm pivot oil seals, and Norton Isolastic shims, he wished he had a bike to work on. But Bert's commitment for this winter was racquetball, and when he returned from McD's with their six fishwiches, he and Scotty sat down on the old couch and focused on Scotty's clipboard.

"Okay," Scotty said. He touched the tip of his pencil to the photocopied drawing of the floor of a racquetball court. "We're gonna start to learn this game by considering the court and where to position ourselves to best advantage." He moved the pencil as he talked.

"The game is played inside a box forty feet long, twenty wide, and twenty high. All surfaces are in play." Scotty took a swig of his Coke. The eight-ounce bottle was tiny in his hand. "Ball comes off the front wall, side wall, ceiling, back wall. It comes from everywhere and at various speeds. We can't control where the ball comes from. But since we know where the ball's going most of the time, we try to control that position on the court."

Bert took a chomp of fishwich. A glob of tartar sauce landed on the court with a soft splat. He made a sheepish face and wiped it off with a napkin.

Scotty looked down. He circled the grease spot, which was equidistant between the side walls and a little back of the receiving line. "We know that the majority of shots bounce right back here." He tapped the pencil in the center of the circle. "Center court, a step back of the receiving line." He looked up again. His face and his voice hardened. "You serve the ball, and you relocate on this spot. You return the ball—no matter where you are on the court—and you get your ass back to this spot. Sure, sometimes the other guy is gonna hit an excellent shot, and you might get to it if you're standin' up by the wall. Sometimes the guy's gonna kill it, too, but you can't return those because they're not hittable. Most of the time the guy is going to leave the ball up." Scotty's voice softened now. "And where's that ball gonna come bouncin'?"

Bert tapped his finger in the center of the grease spot.

"You bet your boots," Scotty said. "And then you're gonna put it away."

Scotty went to work with the pencil again. "Something you've gotta do that goes right along with position," he said, "is watch your opponent." He made an *O* in the back left corner of the court. "This is your opponent," he said. He made a *B* inside the greasy circle. "This is you—the Big B."

Bert smiled. This information was not new to him. He'd read it in *Strategic Racquetball*. But everything was different now. Now he had a coach to focus it for him. If you had a coach you trusted, you could give up your responsibility for the zillions of things there were to think about and just concentrate on what he told you. You could focus all your attention, all your strength and energy on that. He took you step by step down the path. The path led to a field of play where you were on your own, but if you'd been well coached, you were ready.

Bert heard the squeak of the shop van's brakes, and in a minute Rita was pushing through the back door. She held a racquet in her hand. She flipped it to Bert, then she took off her leather jacket and scarf.

Bert held up the racquet. "What's this?"

"That's Rita's racquet," Scotty said. "Grab hold."

Bert did.

"Feel how it fits your hand?"

The handle was thin. Really thin. Bert's small hand felt big around it. He nodded.

EKTELON, the brand, was written on the frame near the handle, and QUANTUS, the model, was written next to it. Bert smiled. It made him think of the Australian airline and their koala bear mascot. A furry little koala

munching eucalyptus was an appropriate symbol for Bert
Bowden to carry into competition.

"The handle on that Head you destroyed was too
thick," Scotty said. "You'll never develop any accuracy,
and you'll never get any smoke on the ball, if you can't
control your racquet. Use Rita's until you get your own."

Bert turned to Rita. "What will you use?" he asked.

"I'm just a banger," Rita replied. "It doesn't matter
what I use."

"Rita's major strength on the court is body checking,"
Scotty said. "Body checking and high sticking."

Scotty and Rita both laughed. Their faces were bright.

Rita had walked to Bert, and now she looked down
at him. "Sometimes Scott and I go full contact," she said.

Rita placed the heel of her hand against Bert's forehead and pulled the tape with her thumb and index finger. Bert felt the tape and bandage lift. "You're going to
have a scar, Bert," she said. "Can your folks afford cos-
metic surgery?"

"I want the scar," Bert said. "I figure a scar might kind
of ease me into a tattoo."

"What's your plan after self-mutilation?" Scotty said.
"A stretch in the state pen?"

"Satanism, maybe," Bert replied. "Maybe heavy metal.
I don't know yet. Maybe aerobics."

Scotty and Rita laughed. Rita sealed the tape with her
thumb.

"I bashed my own head," Bert said. "I'm a psycho."

Rita moved her fingers into Bert's hair. "You're not a psycho, baby," she said. "A psycho bashes someone else's head."

Bert spent his Saturday night whacking away at that little blue ball. He practiced the only two serves he had, a drive and a lob. He hit the ball, then turned and watched it. When the ball crossed the receiving line Bert hustled back to midcourt and set up. He worked that one move again and again. He served, turned, watched the ball cross the line, relocated at midcourt, watched his imaginary opponent set up various returns.

When Bert began to feel like he'd go nuts if he hit one more serve, he hit forehands until he couldn't stand it, then he hit backhands. He was trying to create a fluid motion.

But fluid motion refused to be created. Maybe two of ten forehands felt right, and no backhands. Not a single backhand in ten minutes of hitting felt smooth. It was pathetic.

Bert lost his match on Wednesday. He won one of the games, though, and scored ten and twelve points in the other two. His court position allowed him plenty of good shots, but even with the right racquet he still wasn't accurate enough to put them away. The other guy wasn't good, but he was better than Bert.

Bert felt okay about it. He hadn't given in to any of his

urges to scream, smash his racquet, quit, and go home. It was true that he'd uttered a few nasties under his breath, and it was also true that he was playing with Rita's racquet, which he was not about to break on purpose. Still, he had exercised a degree of self-control.

Thursday evening, before team racquetball, Scotty worked Bert on stroke. Forehand and backhand. "Like you're hitting a baseball" was the phrase Scotty repeated. "Set up solid, stride into the ball, watch your racquet meet it and then, *then* bring your head up. Swing through it in a smooth stroke. The power starts in your shoulder, builds on the downstroke and tops out in the wrist snap. The power needs to exhaust itself, and it does that in the follow-through.

"Meet the ball a little in front of your forward hip," he said. "Don't let the ball get into you. That's what restricts your swing. Forehand, backhand, it doesn't matter. Think of yourself as a switch-hitter, and work to develop a smooth swing from both sides."

Bert's forehands weren't too bad. He thought he had the feel of it. But his backhands were a disaster. He felt like his mind was trying to hit the ball with someone else's body. Scotty said it would come. "One thing in the world you can count on, Bert," he said, "is that practice makes you better. And it makes you better a hell of a lot faster when you're young.

"But a guy's got to have patience," Scotty said. "And

patience is tough, especially when you're young."

Patience, Bert thought. Where have I heard that before?

Scotty stepped closer to the back wall. The leather in his knee braces creaked. He bounced the ball into the corner, then unloaded a backhand. It shot to the front as straight and fast as if he'd faxed it there.

"A guy can get his patience to come a little easier if he reminds himself that his practice will pay off," Scotty said. "It ain't like faith, because this ain't magic. This is plain old cause and effect."

A week later Bert won a match. He lost the third game, but he won the match. It was wild. And it was fun.

Bert had scheduled the match late so Scotty could watch. Steve, who knew Bert's opponent from the weight room, came too.

Three things about the match were amazing to Bert. First: Position *was* an advantage. A huge percentage of the guy's returns came back through that spot at midcourt. And when they didn't, Bert was still able to reach a lot of them by taking that one long cross-step Scotty taught him. Second: Strategy could help him beat a better athlete. After the match the guy told Bert he played football for Whitworth College.

The third thing that amazed Bert was the most important. It was, in fact, one of those life-changing realizations: There were times during the match when Bert was concentrating so hard on *staying home*, on getting back home to that midcourt position and watching his opponent's return, that he forgot Scotty and Steve were watching him. Between points he'd raise his eyes to see if they were still there, and he'd try to read their faces. And sometimes when the speed of the ball slowed, his concentration would lag and self-consciousness would leak into his mind and his only concern would be what Scotty and Steve thought of his play.

But when the game was hot and the ball was steaming, Bert's mind and body were locked into that singular pursuit. If he could keep doing that, and if he kept on learning so he had more knowledge in his head to concentrate on, then maybe he could plug those leaks where self-consciousness seeped in like silt. And maybe then all the potential in him—however much that was—would finally have a chance to flow out through a clear channel. *People who have the guts make it happen*, Scotty had said. Maybe Bert could find the guts, and maybe he could make it happen.

Bert's humility made it easy for him to apprentice himself to Scott Shepard. It was an old-fashioned relationship and it required this old-fashioned quality of character. Bert saw Scotty as a master craftsman. Scotty had knowledge Bert wanted, and Bert was willing to do what Scotty told him to gain that knowledge. He knew Scotty wouldn't hurt him or humiliate him, so he just gave himself up.

This did not mean, however, that Bert was thrilled to be doing aerobics every Monday, Wednesday, and Friday at five-thirty with the hardbodies. Scotty told him he needed conditioning and strength-training. He said aerobics was the best conditioning he knew, and for the strength-training he advised a circuit on the weight machines. In a tournament, Scotty said, you might play three matches a day. And if you also played doubles, it could be five. If a guy wanted to be competitive, he had to be in shape.

Scotty, Steve, and Bert had been sitting in the club's hot tub when Scotty issued this advice. Usually the tub was full of people, but the guys were alone this night, and Steve had taken these moments of privacy to add his counsel to his brother's.

"Aerobics is tough, Bootsie," Steve said. "It's tough—not to mention potentially embarrassing and even dangerous—doing these routines with a boner. Few things in this life are a bigger turn-on than sweaty women in skimpy outfits. Add the Dionysian frenzy that rock and roll produces, give a number of these women the muscle tone of a Rottweiler, and you're talking about a lethal jolt to the gonads. This is not to mention the damage the unfulfilled fantasies can do to your psyche. Particularly for a guy in his sexual prime such as yourself."

Bert had looked at Steve through the mist. Steve thought this was funny. But it was not funny to Bert.

"My advice?" Steve said. "My advice is to pay the

women no mind. If circumstances force you to notice them—say you happen to open your eyes during the hour—just think of them as other athletes getting their work done. After all, that's what they are."

Steve's counsel had been wise, but it didn't help much at first. The aerobics women were athletes, all right, and most of them were better athletes than Bert. Still, it was difficult integrating the beauty of breasts into this concept. The breasts didn't have to be big or firm or clearly demarcated; even a smooth curve resisting the inertia of a floppy sweatshirt could do it. If Bert's eyes locked on to breasts, his clapping would stray off the beat, he'd lose the count, he'd stumble out of step.

The distraction was so intense in those first couple of weeks of aerobics that Bert would grab his towel and wipe his face, hoping to suggest that sweat had dripped into his eyes, then he'd drape the towel over his head and tuck it into the collar of his shirt to form a hood. He would restrict his vision in this way, and he would face forward where the only thing he'd see was the back of the woman in the next row. This worked until the routine changed and that woman bent over. Bert would close his eyes before his vision fused with that tiny string of fabric running between the woman's legs.

Bert's thoughts of sex became so obsessive that he was losing sleep. He would scan the cable guide for movies rated N for nudity and SC for sexual content, and particularly for those rated N, SC, then he'd stay up till three A.M. watching. Bert was literally paralyzed by some of the scenes. Paralyzed except for his hand. He canceled the movie channel while he still had the willpower.

Bert thought of women's breasts as the most beautiful creation in nature. Heavy breasts, smaller breasts hard like apples, breasts that perked up like the faces of playful animals, breasts that sloped like slings full of milk, breasts so slight, they seemed only an outline of themselves and a nipple. They were all beautiful to Bert. There were times when he wanted more than all the other things he wanted in his life just to kiss a woman's breasts.

Steve's advice only began to take hold after Bert started watching how Steve and Scotty treated the women at the club. They not only didn't ogle the women like a lot of the guys, they didn't even acknowledge any difference in them. They looked a woman in the face and said, "How ya doin'?" Their expression was the same whether the woman wore her string leotard or her ski parka, whether she was young or old, attractive or not.

When Bert started acting toward the women the way Steve and Scotty did, he began to feel more at ease in aerobics. If he looked at the women, it was their faces he focused on. If they smiled, Bert smiled back and said, "How ya doin'?" If they didn't, he smiled anyway and went to work.

In addition to his suggestion about aerobics and strength-training, Scotty had also advised Bert to watch certain players. Every time these men and women played they gave a racquetball lesson. Maybe the subject would be court strategy, maybe variety of serves, maybe stroke, maybe superiority with a particular shot, maybe an ability to maintain concentration, maybe grace in competition. Every good player gave lessons, and all you had to do to get one, Scotty said, was check the court reservations to find out when they were playing.

Gary Lawler wasn't among the players Scotty told Bert to watch, but Bert kept an eye on the reservation calendar for Lawler's name, anyway, and he checked his scores in the standings.

Lawler's scores were highest in B league. He was a decent player, but in all the times Bert watched the guy he'd never seen him up against anybody who could really play. One guy had a good drive serve, another was fairly accurate, another really smoked the ball, another had speed and endurance, but none of them did more than one or two things well.

Lawler was quick, and he cheated way up past the serving box. He got to a lot of balls, and he put them away with a pinch shot that was so accurate, it pissed you off even when you weren't down there getting beat by it.

Bert knew it was easy to stand up at the rail and see what was wrong with another guy's game. It was easy to get it right in your head. But it was real hard to get it right when you were down there on the court.

At the end of February, Lawler was still on top in B. Bert had won five straight and moved up to the middle of C. He was feeling strong and wasn't fading in third games.

Bert didn't think he was playing well, though. He'd begun winning just on his knowledge of the game, and this had begun to feel like cheating. Few of the guys in C cared how the game was played. Most of them were working men who wanted to sweat and bang out their frustrations on that blue ball. They played once, twice a week, and they never practiced. Bert played Tuesday, Thursday, Saturday night, and Sunday, and he practiced after aerobics on the other days.

Bert was afraid that the skills of the game were coming too slowly. He told himself to be patient, but that was another thing more easily conceived than enacted.

Bert was suffering a mild case of despair as he and Scotty sat in the hot tub for their Thursday night critique. Earlier Bert had played his best match since league started against the best player he'd faced. He lost the first game 11–15, then won the last two 15–13 and 15–9. Scotty had arrived for game three.

Winning wasn't much of a thrill and neither was having played his best. All he was doing was making fewer mistakes than his opponents. If this was the extent of his best play, where did that put him?

"It puts you, Bert," Scotty said, "at the point where I tell you to give yourself a fucking break."

The tub was full of team racquetball players. Scotty spoke quietly, and against the talk and laughter, the hum of the pump and bubbling of the water, nobody over-heard. But his voice had that edge to it. It was the voice he'd used when Bert bashed his head.

But then his voice softened and rose to a conversational level. "I'll tell you what I mean," Scotty said. "You're at a plateau. You understand a bunch of stuff with your head, but your body hasn't got it yet. It will.

"Here's what I want you to do," he said.

Bert felt a surge of excitement. It was like an electric current pouring in with the jets of water.

"I want you to start hitting the shit out of the ball," Scotty said. "Backhands too. I want you to just blast the fuck out of every ball you hit."

This was more of a jolt than Bert was ready for.

Scotty held his hands up in a gesture that said, Give me a minute here. "In practice hit the ball as hard as you can, and try to do it from a perfect setup through a perfect swing. In practice think about power and about the shape of the human spring that creates it. But in games I don't want you thinking about anything except blasting the ball into powder. I don't care if you skip a hundred balls and get skunked three straight every match until the league ends.

"You know the fundamentals of this game, Bert," Scotty said. "If you add to those things all the strength you've got, and if you give your body some time, it'll create a racquetball player."

Bert closed his eyes and sank to the bottom of the tub.

When his shoulders met the tile he opened his eyes and looked up into the blue luminescence. He let the air in his lungs float him to the surface. "And the second thing?" he said.

Scotty smiled, then he laughed his big, deep laugh. "The second and third things aren't so long-winded," he said. "I want you to get a B-league sheet and start calling some of those people for games."

"Nobody'll want to play me," Bert said. "I'll be pulverizing all the balls."

Scotty laughed again. "Balls are cheap," he said.

"What's last?" Bert said.

"There's a tournament in Richland the second weekend in March," Scotty replied. "I want you to enter the C bracket. If Thompson's basketball team makes regionals they'll be playing there that weekend. Maybe I could get to one of your matches."

"I work Saturdays," Bert said.

Scotty smiled and shook his head.

"But I think my boss will let me off for this."

So Bert proceeded to whale on that little blue ball. And it wasn't pretty. It didn't seem to matter whether he was thinking about power and stroke or about the human spring he was endeavoring to become, the ball seldom went where he meant it to. And it seldom went with power.

It was dangerous to play Bert in this stage of his racquetball evolution. No one, including Bert himself, had a clue where his vicious swings would send the ball, and there was always the chance that he might smoke one. Bert knocked a light-panel out of the ceiling. He hit an untold number of balls out of the court, one of which knocked the headphones off a woman pumping away on the StairMaster. He got too far around on a backhand and actually hit the ball behind him. His opponent was standing across court in the corner, as far from danger as he could get. Still, Bert drilled him.

"Now there's a backhand, kid," the guy said after he pulled up his T-shirt and showed Bert the reddening imprint of the ball over his bottom rib. "The fucking thing goes backward."

Bert got games with some B people. But he didn't call Gary Lawler. He did, however, have Lawler's phone number handy now. And Bert would call. When his game evolved a little more.

Chapter 25

Waiver of Responsibility

Spokane received its last snowfall of winter on the first Tuesday in March. A few light flakes melted against the Bug's windshield as Bert drove to the print shop after fifth period. Scotty was happy to give him these afternoons off so he could work with the *Explorer* staff. Bert helped make up the paper until it was time to head for the club and his five-thirty match. When he walked out the print shop door he stepped into snow higher than his high-tops. The flakes were big and wet. The Bug was all white including the tires.

Bert left his head in the locker room and let his body play the match as the plan dictated. His body lost to a guy his own age from St. George's named Kevin, whom his mind could have beaten. It was okay though. Bert finally smoked a few for points, even one backhand, and he served a few drives for aces. Those shots felt like dreams made flesh, graphite, and nylon, and they sounded—not like high-caliber, but certainly like medium-caliber weapons. They sounded almost like the shots of a real player. Bert stood there after the ball rolled out and wondered who hit it. Kevin looked back and wondered the same.

The Bug wore a twelve-inch snowcap when Bert left

the club to return to the print shop. Darby was the only staffer still there. She said Tanneran left early because he'd taken his snow tires off the day before and was afraid he'd never make it home if he stayed any longer.

Bert was a smart kid, but he didn't know everything, and one of the things he didn't know was that dealing with the sexuality in aerobics class rather than remaining at the mercy of it was, in a subtle way, putting him less at the mercy of sexuality in general. Bert was also unaware that his commitment to racquetball had cut into his self-consciousness; there just wasn't enough room in his head or time in his life to be obsessed with everything. Further, Bert didn't realize that the conditioning he was doing had shaped him up. His body was a little stronger and so supported itself in a more confident posture. Bert's head had not received this message yet, but it would. The culmination of this growth was that—even though he didn't know it—Bert had begun thinking of Darby Granger as just another kid. And so, for the first time since September when he'd seen her in the journalism room through the haze of headache and humiliation and asked her if Tanneran was around, Bert spoke to Darby without being spoken to first.

He was pasting up a story about the controversy over AIDS education in Spokane schools when he stopped and looked at Darby, who was running headlines through the paste machine. "Hey, Darb," Bert said. "Does controversy always have to rage?"

The look she gave him was similar to Kevin's expression on the racquetball court. *You* said something? *You* hit that ball?

"Couldn't controversy maybe *thunder* for a change? Couldn't it *boil* or *fulminate?*"

"We're not poets, Egg," Darby replied. "We're journalists. Clichés are the heart and soul of journalism. They're our meat and potatoes."

"I was just curious," Bert said.

The scar on Bert's forehead was not a major disfiguration, but it did show clearly in the strong lights of the paste-up room and Darby's eyes had been drawn to it all evening. "I'm curious about something too, Egg," she said. "How'd you get the scar?"

Bert told her the truth.

"I had my suspicions about you," Darby said. "You are not just an egg: You are a psycho egg."

"I'm harmless to others" was Bert's response.

It was pushing nine o'clock when Bert finished pasting up the rewrites and Darby had taken care of all the headlines and together they had stacked the pages in the correct order for the printer. Bert took the stack and said he'd carry it to the back room. As he was walking away he stopped. "I'm starved," he said. "You feel like a bite to eat, Darb?"

Bert had spoken before he thought. He wished he could take it back.

But it was too late. Darby said she always felt like a bite

to eat. She also said they'd take her Tracker. She'd hoped all winter for a snow like this so she and the plows could be the only ones on the road.

Bert said he could put away a bunch of fishwiches. Darby heard the suggestion of concern for low cholesterol and wondered if Bert was not only an egg but a health Nazi. She wasn't independent beyond all effects of peer pressure, however, so she mentioned chicken. But Darby Granger wasn't into low cholesterol. She looked over at Bert and said, "You know what I really feel like eating, Egg?"

It was easy for Bert to reply because he also had a hankering. "Greaseburgers!" they said in unison. So Darby pointed the Tracker in the direction of Dick's Drive-in, where Spokane's finest greaseburger is served.

It was strange for Dick's to be so quiet. But then the whole town was quiet. The snow fell so thick, it was like a white string curtain, and it was so wet, it stuck to everything. Even the lights were subdued by a covering of snow. Bert and Darby heard the plows roll by on Division and the big trucks rumble by on the elevated freeway, but even with those sounds it was almost like being out in the country. Darby didn't even have the radio on.

They were down to scouring the last of the tartar sauce out of the little paper cups with the last of the fries when Darby spoke. "Think you want to edit the paper next year?"

Bert looked at her.

"You know, Egg," she said, "edit the *Explorer*. *Be* the editor."

Bert didn't have to think about it. "No," he said. "I'd like to be associate. That's where I'd be the most help." He looked at Darby as he'd look at any friend. "You're an excellent editor," he said. "You're comfortable in authority, people trust your judgment, and you don't humiliate them." He shifted in his seat. "I never thought you were making fun of me when you called me Egg."

"You know why I call you Egg, Bert?" Darby said.

Bert squinched his face. "Because I remind you of something shot out of a chicken's ass?"

Darby smiled. "Besides that," she said. "I call you Egg because you have a shell."

It didn't hurt Bert's feelings. He knew it was true.

The plows had been up Maple Street, so once Darby hooked her nylon tow rope on to the Bug and pulled it out of the print shop lot, Bert was mobile.

The last flakes of the last snow of winter fell before Bert had driven many blocks. The temperature was rising. It must have been above freezing already. Bert wasn't tired and he needed to have one of his parents sign the waiver on his tournament form, so he passed up the turn to Gram's and headed to his folks' house.

He left the Bug in the middle of the street, took the shovel from the porch, and went to work on the driveway. His dad must be out of town. If he were home, he'd be out with his snowblower.

It was so quiet. So quiet and so beautiful. The pine and

fir and spruce trees in the yards were completely covered
with snow—it was like they'd been sprayed. Their lower
branches drooped to the ground under the weight. They
didn't even look like trees. They looked like snow spires.
Serene was the name for this night. Bert's shovel scraping
lightly against the concrete was the only sound. Before
long Bert heard the garage-door opener kick in, then his
mom appeared in her robe and slippers.

They sat at the kitchen table and looked out the window at the woods. Bert dropped little marshmallows into
his mom's hot chocolate until the surface was covered with
white like everything outside, then he covered his own
with a double layer.

Bert assured her that he was feeling fine, that if he were
losing weight, it was because of exercise, not diet or anxiety. He said he was too busy to be anxious.

Jean Bowden was surprised to hear that her son was
doing aerobics. She'd tried aerobics for a while but got frustrated because she couldn't keep up with the routines. She
still had her outfit. Bert said it took a while to get the hang
of it. He said a lot of women her age came to the classes.

Jean asked if Bert was doing okay at Gram's, and he
said he was doing fine. "Don't you get lonely out there in
Gramp's workshop by yourself?" she asked.

"I never get lonely," Bert replied. He realized how that
sounded. "Everything else bothers me," he said. "I just
never get lonely."

Jean Bowden smiled and shook her head. Who was this

boy—this young man—she had carried on her hip? One day she left him at kindergarten with tears running down his face, and now he stops by to shovel snow and says he never gets lonely.

Yes, she thought it would be all right if he drove to Richland to play in a racquetball tournament. She just hoped the roads would be clear. And yes, she would sign the Waiver of Responsibility required of minors.

Bert swung by the post office on his way home. He had to climb out to drop the envelope in the curb box because the plows had buried it in a huge snowpile.

He thought of responsibility the rest of the way home, and he thought of responsibility as he lay in bed.

Bert wondered how his parents could have placed him in the hands of a man like Lawler. They were supposed to be responsible for him, and yet they just handed him over to that prick.

They were trying to be responsible, Bert knew. They were trying. They just fucked up. His dad was gone all the time then, and his mom had just started college. They were busy, and it had just slipped by.

For the first time, Bert realized something: His folks weren't responsible for him anymore. They had waived their responsibility when they stuck him in Lawler's class for a second year. He tried not to blame them for that, but it was tough. He was responsible for himself now. He wasn't crazy about the idea. That's just how it was.

Chapter 26

Letting It Go

Bert exited 395 South at the Richland sign. Gleeful radio voices were forecasting temps in the sixties, maybe as high as seventy by Sunday. What a weekend to ride. Too bad Bert didn't have a motorcycle anymore. He followed the directions on the tournament flyer clipped to his clipboard on the seat beside him, and by God if he didn't wind up at the Tri-Cities Racquet Club. He'd never been on a trip by himself before. So far it was fun.

Bert checked in at the tournament desk and picked up his T-shirt. On the back was written in black TRI-CITIES RACQUET CLUB PRO-AM. He traded his car keys for a locker key and a towel. On his way to the locker room he passed a long table with pastries, apple and orange slices, and two big thermos jugs of juice. God, he thought, I get a shirt worth ten bucks, I can eat maybe five bucks' worth of breakfast now and tomorrow, there's pizza tonight, plus, I get to play racquetball—at twenty-five bucks this is cheap fun. Bert had forgotten for the moment that he would also be paying around forty dollars for the motel.

Bert had been dubious about the workout clothes his mom bought him. He'd found the Nordstrom box on his cot yesterday after school. Two pairs of those shiny, tight knee-length pants, black and neon-blue, and two tank tops cut deep under the arms. He liked the pants, but he couldn't wear the tanks in public. A guy's got to have lats to wear tanks cut like that. Bert had lats, of course; they just weren't developed enough to show.

He wore the blue pants, which were so tight he didn't need a jock, and over them a pair of gold Thompson High PE shorts slit up the sides. He wore an old blue Lacoste shirt, faded and soft. His new Ektelon Quantus racquet was also blue. Bert knew he was going to get murdered in the tournament, but at least he'd get murdered looking good. He hoped, however, that he didn't look too color-coordinated.

Bert did get murdered in his first match. He lost 6–15, 9–15 to a guy named Dirk. Bert remembered the name because he repeated it. "Nice shot, Dirk. Jesus, Dirk, you smoked that one."

Dirk was shaped like a giant ham and had a ham's low fat-content. And he hit the ball as hard as Scotty. He wasn't accurate and all he had was his forehand, but it didn't matter. A lot of times he hit the ball so hard, it bounced off the back wall to the front again before Bert could get to it. Bert would watch him set up, then sometimes before he could turn his head the ball would crack against the front wall and rebound past him.

Bert didn't play badly, he just didn't get a chance to

hit many balls. He was frustrated about that, but still it had been a fun match.

The loss dropped Bert into the consolation round. He checked the chart and learned that he played someone named Stone at three. If he won, he played again at seven. If he lost, the tournament was over for him.

After his shower Bert drove to a strip of motels. He was going to stay the night even if he didn't play in the morning. They all looked clean from the outside, so he stopped at the Blue Mountain Inn because he liked the name.

The girl at the desk saw Bert's bag and asked if he was a racquetball player. He felt like saying only time would tell, but this girl was cute and he didn't want to be a dink. The tag on her blouse said her name was Markie, but Bert figured he would be an even bigger dink if he called her by name. "Yes" was all he said.

He wrote a check for thirty-six dollars, the tournament players' rate, and grabbed his key. As he walked across the lobby he wondered if Markie worked late tonight. He saw himself returning still a little flushed from a tough win. Markie would be walking out. Their eyes would meet and she'd touch his arm. *Nine ½ Weeks* is playing on cable tonight, she'd say. Can we watch it together in your room? Naked?

"Good luck, Albert!" Markie called.

"Thank you!" Bert called back. Why didn't I get "Bert" printed on my checks? he asked himself.

Bert wondered if he would ever have the guts to make a move on a girl. He wondered further if fantasies as pathetic as his grew only in the semen-drenched loam of male adolescence, or if grown-up men also suffered this sexual yearning.

Sam Stone was a wrestler at Columbia Basin College, and everything about him was tough. Bert was even intimidated by his name. The timbre of his voice alone caused Bert to give thanks that racquetball wasn't a combat sport.

But Bert was tough too—at least his drive serve was. And Stone's backhand was wimpy. Bert took the first game 15–4.

Bert was ahead 11–6 in the second game when he began thinking how neat it was to be winning a tournament match. Stone, who was steaming like a rock in a sauna, tied it up. Each broke the other's serve at 14–14 until Bert choked and skipped a backhand.

Bert served first in the tie breaker because he had the most points in the two games. Tie breakers went to eleven. Bert was nervous. He tried to let the feeling go as Scotty had told him. He took a couple of deep breaths at the service line and thought of the nervousness floating away with his exhalations.

It worked. Or something did. And it wasn't just his drive serve again. Bert was all over Stone's returns. He pinched backhands into the corners, he rolled out a couple of forehands, he caught Stone cheating up and went to the ceiling with shots Stone wasn't able to peel off the wall with his backhand.

Bert was stunned when it was over. "That was luck," he said as they shook hands. "I can't play that well."

"You play real tough, kid," Stone said.

Bert would never have said it to anyone, but by that evening he felt like a tournament vet. He'd lost a match, won a match, and reffed a match. In an hour or so he would be finished for the evening, and he would eat as much pizza as he could choke down. He might even draw a short beer from the keg if nobody looked weird at him.

It didn't take nearly an hour. Bert won his evening match 15–2 and 15–10. When he checked the chart he discovered that tomorrow at ten he'd play in the consolation finals. The winner got a trophy. He'd seen it on display.

He listened to Thompson win its regional championship game through his headphones as he watched an open-division match after his shower. They'd beaten Sunnyside in a squeaker the night before. According to the radio announcer, Camille Shepard took a rebound with a few seconds left and flung it over his head into open court. Jackson caught up with it and laid it in. Bert had turned off his radio after the announcer began talking about Camille's triple-double. He had twelve rebounds and ten assists. Bert hadn't wanted to know the point total. Tonight they were blowing out Columbia.

Games were going on in all the courts, but most people sat near the glass walls of court six watching the open match. Workout bags with rows of gloves fastened to their carrying straps and racquet handles protruding from inside were strewn thick as luggage in a snowbound airport. One of the tiny kids toddling around fell into a big open bag and began to howl. The bag's owner grabbed the kid and passed it through the crowd toward a set of outstretched arms.

Plastic cups of beer and pop were also passed, as well as pizza slices. Thin filaments of cheese hung from clothing, hair, and racquet handles like edible gossamer. All this needed to qualify as a picnic would be dogs jumping after Frisbees, Bert thought. Or one of these little kids getting stung by a wasp.

Bert's high spirits had sunk. His stomach was in a nervous froth about tomorrow's match, and he was ashamed of being jealous of Camille Shepard. He wondered if you could grow to become generous in your heart or if you had to be born that way.

Bert drank a lot of pop, but he didn't put away as much pizza as he'd envisioned. It was fun being with all the players and their families, but it would have been more fun if he'd known someone.

Markie was still at the motel desk, looking as unsullied as a new ball right out of the can. "How'd you do, Albert?" she asked.

"I did okay, Markie," Bert replied. "I get to go back and play again tomorrow."

"All right!" Markie said.

Bert knew it wasn't personal, but still he felt like thanking her for her interest. "Good night" was his response.

On the way to the club Bert began to wish Scotty would show up, but by the time he arrived he was glad no one who knew him would be there. It was the same feeling he'd had when he was little. He wanted his dad to come to his games, but he didn't want his dad to see him screw up. Bert's dad was always traveling, though, or too tired from having traveled, so he never saw Bert play.

The only person watching as Bert got set to receive the serve was the ref, a woman who had won a consolation final earlier. Bert's opponent was a slight man in his fifties named Angie Priano. He looked particularly distinguished in his tennis whites. Bert was moved to call him sir, but he didn't.

Angie had a good lob serve, but Bert was patient with it and his backhand was on. His drive serve was on too. Everything was on. Bert won the first game 15–9.

Bert served first in game two. He looked back to see if Angie was ready, then he looked up. The entire wall was filled with Thompson people. Camille was there, and Mike, Krista, Darby, and Sean. Bert saw a 35mm camera resting on the wall edge with Mark Schwartz's frizzy red hair like an explosion behind it. The Hmongster was mounting a video camera on a tripod. Steve was there, and Zimster beside him, just high enough in his chair to see over the wall. Scotty stood on one side of the ref, and Rita on the other. "Zero serves zero," the ref said.

Bert was a different player in game two. He played with desperation, rather than exuberance. Despair and joy are opposite emotions, but some of the behaviors they produce look almost the same. It's a subtle difference, and maybe only Scotty and Steve recognized it. Bert knew it too. He knew exactly what was happening to him, but he couldn't stop it. He hustled, he kept the rallies going. But Angie was the one with the touch this game, and he ended the majority of them. Angie was also the one with fifteen points. Bert had ten.

Ten points is a respectable score, but to Bert it had been a disgraceful performance. He walked out of the court and wanted to keep going. But there was nowhere to go. He had to be back in two minutes to humiliate himself again in the tie breaker.

Bert had only taken a couple of steps when Scotty wrapped an arm around his shoulder. Angie walked by breathing hard. "No coaching," he said. He was smiling. "The kid's doing just fine."

"My boy's unraveling out there," Scotty said. "Time to take him in hand."

Scotty told Bert to grab his towel and gave him a little push in the direction of his bag. They wove their way through the people sitting and lying on the floor to the quietest corner. Scotty leaned against the wall. He put his hand on Bert's head and tapped him just lightly with his index finger. "Whatever's in there that does this to you, Bert," he said, "it's time to let it go." He withdrew his hand.

Bert was still sweating. He wiped his face again and looked up at Scotty.

"When you walk through that door this time," Scotty said, "I want you to forget everything in your life but the racquetball you've learned. Give yourself to the game. Don't think about us watching, and don't think about your opponent. The competition ain't between you and him. It's between you and the game. You guys are in there to make the game more fun for each other."

Scotty held Bert's head again and shook him just lightly. "Your opponent is that shit in your head," he said. "Let it go, son."

"I'll try," Bert said.

Bert was up on total points so he had the serve in the tie breaker. He looked back to see if Angie was ready. He looked up at the ref. He looked at the people who'd come to watch him play. He turned back and looked at the blue ball. What he saw was himself as a little kid in his pre-Lawler days. A little kid playing sports and having fun. And doing both things well.

It took a few exchanges of serve for Bert to loosen up. He heard voices from above, he heard his own voice in his head. But the more he followed that blue ball with his eyes and his body and his will, the more everything but the ball went away. And after a while the blue ball was everything.

He listened for the score, but he didn't hear it as a comment on his character. It was a comment on the game.

At 3–3 Bert felt loose and strong. He fired up his drive serve. He dropped the ball as he strode forward, his head low and his eyes locked, his arm rising with the stride, then coming down to meet the ball as his front foot planted. When he saw the ball pass the receiving line, he relocated and watched. Just like in practice.

But this was more fun than practice because some-body was there to hit it back. Sometimes. The ball was coming pretty hard, and Angie didn't return them all. When he did, Bert was there. He drilled a couple back-hands cross-court that Angie didn't get near. The smooth-ness of the motion was like a dream. Or like something remembered.

At 9–3 Bert served to Angie's forehand. The ball caught the crack for an ace. "Lucky shot," Bert said.

Angie smiled. The kid was hitting a lot of lucky shots.

"Match point serving three," the ref announced.

Bert thought he might sneak another one by up the right side. But this was what Angie was expecting. He was set up, and he hit it cross-court. Hard.

Bert was after it, raising his racquet as he moved so he'd be ready to swing if he got the shot. He saw that the ball was going to hit the side wall. And it was going to hit real low. He planted his front foot as he watched it hit, and he swung at the spot where he thought it would come off.

And he connected. The ball hit the front wall a few inches from the floor, and that was the match. It was a sweet shot. It had been as good a shot as Bert was capable of hitting. It was also lucky, but that didn't make it any less sweet.

Angie held out his hand and they shook. Bert heard the cheers. He didn't want to look up, but he couldn't help himself. He looked down again right away.

The sound rang in his ears all the way home.

Chapter 27

Phantom Pleasure, Phantom Pain

Lawler won the B league and moved up to A. He was out of range for now, but Bert kept him in his sights. Lawler was good; Bert wasn't kidding himself about that. He had a couple of excellent lob serves and a pinch shot he hit from all over with his forehand or backhand. No, he didn't hit it from all over—that was the point. He only hit it from the receiving line or closer. Lawler's game was narrow. Bert believed that a player with a wider range of skills who could play the whole court—maybe even an inferior player, such as Bert himself—could get Lawler out of his game and beat him.

So Bert kept watch on Lawler. He continued to watch the best players in the club, too, but a lot of these guys didn't come around after the weather warmed up. They golfed, Scotty said, or fished or played softball or worked around the house.

The player Bert watched most often now was himself—thanks to Cheng Moua. It took the Hmongster three weeks to edit the video he shot at the Richland tournament. He walked into the journalism room on a Monday noon rolling a cart with a VCR and a monitor and wearing a confident smile. "Showtime!" he announced. "Championship racquetball. Bert Bowden versus some old Italian guy. Admission is free."

It was like a how-to film, and a how-not-to film as well. The Hmongster had split the screen and shown Bert hitting backhands on the left side and forehands on the right. This was intercut with the progress of the match and comments from the people watching. The concluding sequence was Bert's backhand kill, Camille Shepard yelling "Smokin' backhand!," Bert and Angie shaking hands, and then Bert looking up for half a beat before he looked back down again. The final frame was Bert's lowered head with Zimster's voice-over. "He used to be a really good athlete when we were kids. I guess he's found his sport."

It was a lot more than a racquetball lesson, really: It was a story about Bert.

Cheng gave Bert a copy, and Bert bought him a three-pack of tapes in return. Now Bert could watch himself play racquetball, and he did this often.

The focus of attention around Thompson High in the spring—and the reason Bert had the journalism room all to himself at lunch now—was Camille Shepard's band. This was also the subject of *The Explorer's biggest* story since the basketball team took second place in state. It was so big that Darby covered it herself. Every noon she was down in the band room watching rehearsals and auditions for the "show" part of the "dance and show" that Shepard had given his word would revolutionize the concept of senior proms.

When Darby had first mentioned the story at a staff meeting, Schwartz instantly piped up. "Wait a minute. Shepard is going to learn to play an instrument and put together a band for a 'dance and show' by May twenty-sixth? He's going to sandwich this in between genetic research and mediating ethnic disputes in the Balkans, I guess."

Bert wanted to laugh. He was glad Schwartz had been the one to make the crack.

"He's been playing the piano since he was a little kid," Darby replied. "He started guitar when he was twelve." She turned to Bert. "How come you didn't get any music stuff in your story on him, Egg?"

"He didn't say a word about music."

"The Shepster is a modest fellow," Schwartz said.

Schwartz was being sarcastic, but Bert had to concede that Camille really was modest.

"You guys have to see him," Darby said. "You won't believe it."

"The boy can play, all right," Cheng said.

This news sent Bert's envy meter to the red line, but it also intrigued him. How could a guy be a kick-ass guitar player and go for almost an entire school year without letting anybody know he played?

Bert knew that Scotty played in a band on Saturday nights, but Scotty had never said anything about Camille playing. Bert preferred not to think about Camille Shepard. He didn't like facing Shepard's illustration that so much was possible in one life. It made him feel ashamed of how little he himself had accomplished and was accomplishing, and it made him envious of Shepard's gifts. Bert wanted to concentrate on using his own modest gifts to pursue his own modest goals, so this is where he focused his mental and physical energy.

And Bert's body responded. It had been responding all along at its own pace, in the way healthy bodies work when we set a task for them.

But Bert's body began doing weird things as well. It made him think of the phantom pains people suffer when they lose a limb. Except that this wasn't painful. It felt good.

Bert would be sitting in class reading, his hands holding the book, his shoulders square. And then he would feel himself turn sideways, his leading shoulder dip, his arm pull the racquet back high, his front foot stride into the ball. He would even feel the contact. The vibrations would run up his arm.

Bert sat still as a stone while some dimension of him played racquetball. His shoulders dipped into forehands and backhands, his wrist snapped at contact, his legs took that one long cross-step to get him to the ball. It was weird, but it was neat, too.

The pain began when Bert felt his arms reach wide for the handlebars of a motorcycle. When he felt the vibration of the engine go up his thighs and into his throttle hand. When he felt the wind in his face. This wasn't a physical pain; but it was a pain of loss. He wasn't a Harley guy, but he must be a motorcycle guy of some kind. His body wanted to ride.

Not long after these feelings began, Bert's body actually started moving with them. As he slept his hips would rotate, his shoulders roll, his feet move to setup, his hand close around a racquet handle, around the throttle of a motorcycle.

Chapter 28

A Norton Guy

Daylight saving time had kicked in and Bert was still without a motorcycle to save daylight for. He began suffering serious withdrawal by the end of April. Bikes were everywhere. The Japanese crotchrockets zipped by like angry bees, and the Harleys roared like artillery shells. Bert spread his hands wide on the steering wheel, twisting his right hand as though he held a throttle. He made motor sounds with his lips. He leaned his head out the window to feel the rushing air and the sharp kiss of winged insects.

Bert didn't care if motorcycles weren't on the official list of human needs. He needed a bike, and he was going to buy one. He had twelve hundred bucks left from the sale of the Sportster. If Scotty couldn't find a cheap classic bike soon, he'd buy a restored one. If he couldn't afford something that nice, he'd go Japanese. This was Bert's emotional state as he walked across Highway 2 from the parking lot of Rosauers Foods on the morning of the first Saturday in May.

The first thing Scotty said was "Got something to show ya."

They walked through the shop and out the back door to the van. Scotty extended his arm toward the open cargo door. There sat a Norton Commando rolling chassis with engine and transmission bolted down. "The rest of it's in the crates."

Behind the bike sat four milk crates. One held a yellow Commando gas tank.

"A 1973 Norton Commando," Scotty said. "This is the deal we've been looking for. I rebuilt this engine and did the Isolastics the first year we were in Spokane. The guy was going to do the rest, but he never got to it. Now he's headed back for California. He was happy to get five hundred bucks. Just for fun I dug up the work order. It cost him almost a grand then. The bill would be twice that now."

"And I can buy this motorcycle?" Bert asked.

"You must buy this motorcycle," Scotty replied. "This bike is you. I suspected all along you might be a Norton guy, and now I know. That Sportster was just a transitional ride."

Bert took the Norton home to Gram's in the shop van. In its dismantled condition it was easy to unload alone. He yearned to piece through the crates, but Scotty needed him back at the shop.

Throughout his workday, his weight circuit, and his drills on the court Bert thought of the Norton and the crates full of parts. He'd been tempted to skip workout and dive right into bike work, but he was afraid to cheat on his routine. He was afraid that if he skipped a day, he wouldn't deserve to keep making progress. As much as Bert loved bikes, he loved who he was becoming more. He tried to lose himself in the physical exertion, but he couldn't.

When Bert got back home he lost himself in Norton parts. He found a factory shop manual and a Commando parts list in one of the crates, and he checked each piece against the list and set it out on Gramp's workbench. He made notes on his clipboard.

Most of the stuff was there. He was missing the drive chain, battery, muffler brackets, exhaust lock-rings, a rear brake cable, and a stop lamp-switch. Nothing big.

Among the treasures Bert found in the milk crates was an original Norton tool kit, including the little Lucas feeler gauge-screwdriver, and a 750 Commando rider's manual. The cover was greasy and a few of the pages had come unglued, but it was in pretty good condition for its age. Which, Bert realized, was seventeen years, the same age as his own.

Bert was thrilled with all of this right down to the nuts and washers he dug out of the folds of the newspapers in the bottoms of the crates. He couldn't stand still. He felt like calling the company when he saw their number printed on the first page of the rider's manual. NORTON VILLIERS LTD., it said. MARSTON RAOD, WOLVERHAMPTON, WV2 4NW, ENGLAND. TEL. 22399.

They went out of business a few years after they made this motorcycle, Bert thought, and that's a long time ago. What if I called this number? Maybe I'd get some old Brit biker in the Twilight Zone.

It was after midnight when Bert turned out the light

and locked the garage. Tomorrow night he'd start putting his Norton together.

He peed in the grass, then washed his hands, face, and neck with water from the spigot. He grabbed the towel he kept in his room, then stepped back outside to dry himself. It was a beautiful night. Sleeping would be tough. He was too excited.

Chapter 29

Bert Bowden Calling

Bert loved riding his Norton. He loved the sound, which was softer than the Sportster but hard enough. He loved the way the suspension allowed the bike to rise with increased throttle like a living thing breathing deeper as it ran. And he loved knowing he'd put a lot of it together himself. He loved it too much to ride it to school. He didn't want to know what other kids thought of it. What he thought of it was most important.

He rode the Norton to the shop on Tuesday, and when work was over he rolled it up on a workstand. He fit the mercury gauge to the carburetors and saw that they weren't in sync. Scotty observed from over his shoulder. Bert adjusted the throttle stop screws and then the pilot air screws in each carb. When the levels of mercury in the two tubes were even, Scotty gave Bert's shoulder a tap. "You've got it," he said. "Can't dial 'er in any closer than that."

All the Norton needed now was a luggage rack, and after Bert lowered the stand he walked into the showroom, pulled one off the wall, and put the money in the cash register. Scotty walked with him as he pushed the Norton out into the alley.

"I saw the final league standings," Scotty said.

"It's a weak league in spring," Bert said. He'd won B by a few points.

"It's not that weak."

"I'm starting to hit it by people is all," Bert said. "Nobody looks for cross-court stuff. They stand up on the service line and think it's gonna bounce right to 'em."

"I think you should move up to A in June," Scotty said. "Those guys look for everything. And you need to start playing guys who hit the ball."

Bert made a doubtful face. "I s'pose," he replied.

Bert rode to the club with his workout bag and the luggage rack strapped to the back of the seat with bungee cords. It was a beautiful afternoon. The sky was a little lighter blue than a racquetball. Every cloud in the southern sky was tapered on its leading end, and this quality made them appear to have a shared destination. The clouds made Bert think of a herd of animals grazing. They looked like big, contented animals up there.

Bert felt light as a cloud, which was funny because he also felt full. He was full of good feelings. He was on his way to play the winner of C league. The winner of this match played the winner of A league for the club championship. Everyone knew it wasn't the real club championship because spring leagues were so weak, but still it was something.

Bert wasn't as nervous as usual. Part of it was that

he'd been playing well and knew he could probably win this match with his serve alone, and part of it was simply that he was happy. Bert didn't think that even beating Lawler—in spite of the many nights he dreamed it point by point—would make him feel any better than he felt right now.

The playoff matches were two games to fifteen and a tie breaker, but Bert's didn't get that far. He hit drive serves and played strategically in the first game and won it 15–6. He won the second serving a variety of lobs, which worked better than his drives had the first game, and practicing the overhand shots and splat shots he'd been working on with Scotty.

He also practiced staying loose, having fun. Weird to think a guy would have to practice that, but Bert did. When he was loose, when he was absolutely out of himself and into the game—when he was playing *unconscious*—was when he came closest to getting it right. And sometimes he actually got it right.

Bert put in his time on the abdominal machine and was home before dark. It was his responsibility to call Lawler because he was the one challenging upward. He'd taken the number from the A sheet a long time ago. It was the first note he put by his phone when he installed it. And now he was going to dial that number. Hard to believe. Incredible. Amazing. Astonishing. This was the dream of the last five years of his life, and he hadn't even known it until a few months ago. And then he'd committed himself to make it happen. And he did it. I did it, Bert thought as he touched the numbers. I fucking did it.

Bert hadn't heard that voice for five years, but he could have picked it out of a concert crowd. "Gary Lawler," he said. "It's Bert Bowden calling about racquetball. We need to set a time for our playoff game."

Bert had stumbled through his first few calls to guys for games, but then a guy had called him and said pretty much what he'd just said to Lawler. It was confident but friendly, and it was short, so Bert started using it himself.

"How about Saturday morning?" Lawler said.

Bert had wondered if Lawler would recognize his name. "Needs to be early for me," he said. "I work at nine."

"Let's make it six-thirty, then."

"Six-thirty," Bert said. He said good-bye, but Lawler had already hung up. I'll bet he does remember me, Bert thought.

He took his tape player and some favorite tunes to the garage. Clapton, Seger, Dire Straits, Dylan, Eagles, John Cougar Mellencamp. Tunes to mount a luggage rack by. He worked slower than he needed to while both sides played through. Then he roared off through the blue dusk. It wasn't long before he was rolling back under the carport and then letting Gram's screen door bang behind him.

"Where'd you ride off to, Berty?" Gram said.

"Had to test my new luggage rack," Bert replied. "He held up a Baskin-Robbins bag. "It carries ice cream," he said. "That was my prime concern."

Bert ate peanut butter and chocolate out of the quart container. He ate it all. Gram ate a little of her pint of chocolate mousse royale. Bert sat awhile, then gave Gram a kiss and said he was off for a ride. She asked if he had schoolwork, and he said he'd hit it when he got back. "Berty," she said, "I want you to promise me."

He promised.

It was close to ten, but Bert rode in just a T-shirt. He did, however, have his jacket strapped to the rack. He wished Darby Granger were on behind him. It probably wouldn't hurt to call her sometime. She had a boyfriend, but a call from her associate editor for next year wouldn't be out of line. Bert would be patient about Darby and about romance in general. He wasn't confident about a great number of things, but he was fully confident in his belief that everything of value took patience to acquire.

Bert swung by the 7-Eleven, though, just in case Darby was there hoping he'd show up to take her for a ride. But he didn't see her as he rolled past the gas pumps. The only patrons were some Thompson sophomores sitting on the curb eating Cheetos.

He rode south, then east along the Spokane River. Soon the houses thinned out. It was darker here and he could see the stars. Plenty of people cruising. Mostly kids. Boyfriends and girlfriends, some of them on bikes. Ninjas, Interceptors, Katanas—those bikes that are supposed to be so distinctive but are really just stamps of one another. A few Harleys.

Cars were parked at every turn-out. Bert's contemporaries into heavy petting. But maybe they'd only pulled off to look at the stars through the pine boughs, or at the black flowing river. Maybe they'd come here from Dick's with burgers and fries and a contempt for the dangers of cholesterol. More likely, however, they were doing the nasty with flagrant disregard for its consequences. They were doing the bad thing, all right. Everybody was but him. How Bert longed for the opportunity to make such mistakes. How does a guy be patient about a primal urge?

Thank the powers of creation for Bowdenland.

He turned south on Argonne Road and was back among the houses and streetlights. He turned west on Trent and pointed the Norton for home. He slowed at Latus Motors, Spokane's Harley dealership, and looked through the windows at the new bikes.

Bert dipped south onto Sprague and cruised the tattoo parlor. He thought of having RIDE FAST, LIVE

FOREVER written in blue on his throttle arm like Scotty
and Steve and Camille Shepard. The words rang to him
like a statement of faith. Bert wished he could face his
life with such audacity. If he ever had anything written
on his body, this imperative would be it.

Chapter 30

Young Mr. Bowden Strikes Back

Friday night Bert is too nervous to sleep. He tries reading to tire his eyes, he tries lifting the lid of his mind and allowing the nervousness to float away. He watches *Terminator*, *Aliens*, and *Predator* until the sky begins to lighten. He makes coffee then, but can't drink it.

As he rides to the club he tells himself it's just another match. But he doesn't convince himself. Bert Bowden knows a pathetic, futile, desperate, chickenshit lie when he tells himself one. This is not just another match. If he wants to win it, though, he needs to make it one.

Bert is sitting on the steps when one of the strength instructors arrives to open up. Lawler walks through the door as Bert is getting his towel and locker key.

The locker room is silent. Bert has never been here when rock radio wasn't pouring from the various speakers. He is bending to set his helmet on the floor of his locker when "Young Mr. Bowden!" makes him jump.

It sounds like a rooster's crow. Bert turns and watches Lawler walk by the sinks. He holds his chin high and his chest out like a little rooster. Bert would love to let the air out of this guy.

"Young Mr. Bowden," Lawler says as he tosses his bag

down beside a locker. "I remember the name now that I see you. You were one of mine."

"Yup," Bert replies. He sees Lawler in the center of the line of kids walking back from recess, everybody with their arms entwined, singing. Everybody but him and Zimster. Bert sees it as though it took place minutes ago instead of years. He hears kids shouting as they take off down the slide. He hears the creak of chains as kids pump high on the swings. Bert walks out to the courts with the singing voices of his fifth-grade classmates in his ears and their backs and entwined arms in his vision.

He hits a few easy forehands and tries to feast his ears on the pop of the ball. As he hits a little harder and the pop gets a little louder he thinks he feels it nudging out the other sounds in his head. He hears Lawler warming up in another court. He watches his racquet meet the ball, he watches the ball contact the wall and bounce. Bert tries to fill his head with these sensations.

Lawler raps his racquet on the door and pushes through. "Let's get this done," he says. "Two games to fifteen, tie breaker to eleven. Lag for serve."

"Let's do it," Bert says.

He tosses Lawler a new ball. He tries to take deep, even breaths, but his stomach is banging up against his diaphragm. He watches Lawler's lag hit the wall and arc back. He watches it bounce a few inches from the line. Bert reaches out with every sensory receptor for the sight and the sound of that blue ball. His lag isn't bad, but Lawler's was closer.

"Zero serves zero," Lawler says.

Bert can't get a breath. Lawler's drive bounces out of the corner fat. But Bert hits it into the floor with his frame.

"One serves zero," Lawler says.

Don't do this to yourself, Bert thinks. You can play this game. Play it.

This drive is harder and better placed, but Bert takes it about six inches off the floor and right to the ceiling. It bounces back hugging the wall. A beautiful shot. Beautiful and lucky. Bert locates at center court and watches Lawler set up. He swings a smooth, high backhand but gets mostly wall. "Touch shot," Bert says.

"Nice return," Lawler says.

"Zero serving one," Bert says. He's developed an effective drive serve down the right side. He doesn't have a lot of respect for Lawler's backcourt shots, and few guys look for the first serve of the game to come to their forehand, so he lets it go. And it's a sweet one, hugging the wall all the way to the corner.

"Screen," Lawler says.

Bert looks at him. Screen? he thinks. I'm standing in the middle of the court. That serve didn't come within five feet of me. But what he says is "Second serve," and lobs it in the same direction.

Lawler hits a leisurely ceiling shot to what he figures will be Bert's backhand. But the ball is three feet off the side wall and the bounce doesn't carry high enough over Bert's head. Bert takes it overhand and buries it in the right corner. Lawler looks at him as though he's spoken in a foreign language.

One serving one: Bert drives to Lawler's backhand. Lawler waits for it to bounce and gets a solid hit on it. Bert doesn't locate as far back for Lawler as he does for harder hitters, and he sees by his feet that he's coming straight down the wall. Bert is waiting for the ball as it bounces back across the short line. He takes it cross-court with an off-speed backhand. No use for Lawler to go after it, and he doesn't.

Two serving one: Bert's drive takes a crazy bounce out of the corner. Lawler is set up, but only Plastic Man could hit this. "Lucky serve," Bert says.

Lawler shakes his head.

Three serving one: Bert sets up so it looks like he's driving to Lawler's forehand as he did with his first serve of the game, but he goes to his backhand. Lawler is moving to the right side of the court as the ball zips by behind him and bounces out of the left corner. "Nice serve," Lawler says.

"Thanks," Bert replies. He's trying not to think of the score as anything but the announcement of serve. He's trying not to get excited.

Four serving one: Bert hits a good drive and Lawler hits a good return that Bert barely gets his backhand on. Bert doesn't see the ball at first, but he sees Lawler setting up near the service line on the right side. Pinch! Bert tells himself, and he takes off for where he thinks the ball will end up. Lawler pinches it into the right corner. It's a good shot, but Bert's there to take it shoelaces-high and powder it. "Bounced right to me," he says.

Five serving one: Bert faults, then lobs his second serve. Lawler goes to the ceiling. It comes back high along the wall. Bert is lucky just to keep it in play. Lawler pinches it in.

One serving five: Lawler's drive is hard but not low enough. Bert couldn't have asked for a sweeter bounce if he'd dropped the ball himself. Cross-court backhand. Smoke. By the time Lawler has turned to see how Bert will take it, the ball is by him, off the wall and up the right side of the court. "You're no B player," Lawler says.

"Lucky shots," Bert says.

Five serving one: Bert feels in control of the game. He doesn't believe Lawler can get the ball by him. If Lawler's going to score, he's going to have to kill the ball. Bert isn't giving Lawler anything. He isn't serving aces, but his drives are hard and low, and Lawler isn't getting set up. Bert plays the offensive racquetball he and Scotty have been working on. He tries to put away every shot, and for the next seven points he does. Then he skips probably the easiest forehand he's had all game.

It's one serving twelve, but Lawler doesn't announce the score. He's through giving Bert low stuff, and he goes to a backhand lob Z. The first two are perfect, bouncing high off the receiving line and into the side wall. Bert hits the first one straight up into the ceiling and dribbles the second off the wall. The third comes back too high. Bert takes it off the wall with his backhand and tries to bury it. It hits a foot off the floor, but that's too high when the server is planted on the service line. Lawler pinches it into the corner. The swing and the look on his face suggest he's about to close the book on young Mr. Bowden, the lucky little shit.

Four serving twelve: another good lob Z, and another well-hit but strategically stupid return by Bert. Lawler takes it knee-high and puts it away.

You can't get it by him, Bert thinks. Don't try to get it by him. Move him off the service line.

Five serving twelve: another good lob Z, but there's room to return it. Bert takes a breath and waits. He hits a smooth backhand to the ceiling. Lawler goes to the ceiling, Bert goes to the ceiling, Lawler goes to the ceiling. But Lawler's shot is a little hard and he doesn't tuck it in close enough to the wall. Bert sets up a forehand from near the backhand corner. He watches the ball drop down off the back wall, and when it's maybe six inches from the floor he swings. That's the line the ball travels to the front wall. "Fuck," Bert hears Lawler mutter. Let's open that book again, Bert thinks.

Twelve serving five: Just play the game, Bert tells himself. Go with what's working. So he hits the drive. Lawler's return is way up. It comes off the front wall about shoulder-high. Bert can let it go to the back wall and take it on the rebound. But he cuts it off. The ball hits the front wall and is down before Lawler can take a step. He was forty feet away. He couldn't have gotten to the ball in a car. But Lawler is steaming into forecourt, anyway. His momentum carries him to the front wall where he leans to get his breath. He's still facing the wall when he says, "What the fuck kind of racquetball shot is that?"

Bert doesn't consider that Lawler's question might be rhetorical. "The books say to cut off the ball if your opponent's at the back wall," Bert replies.

Lawler walks up to Bert and stands close. "You're still a smartmouth," he says. "You still think you know everything there is to know." Bert steps out of his way.

Thirteen serving five: If they were anywhere but on a racquetball court, Bert would be intimidated. He'd be jelly. But they are on a court, and here it doesn't matter what the asshole says. This world revolves around the blue ball. The blue ball makes the rules, and the blue ball plays no favorites. What Lawler thinks of Bert doesn't mean shit. Bert makes sure he's in the middle of the service zone. Plenty of room for a drive up the right side. Plenty of room for Lawler to see the ball. So Bert drives the ball into the right corner. It's not a great serve, but it doesn't matter because Lawler is nowhere near it. "Screen serve," Bert hears him say.

Bert doesn't think. He just turns. "Screen?" he says. "I'm in the middle of the fucking service zone. That's not a screen."

"That's it," Lawler says. "I'm not playing with a foul-mouthed kid who doesn't even know the game."

"What?" Bert says.

"Get a ref, I'll play," Lawler replies. "Get a ref and give me a call."

"What?" Bert says. But Lawler is walking out the door. In all Bert's dreams of their match it never ended like this.

It was another frenzied Saturday at Shepard's Classic and Custom. Bert stewed about the match all morning. He'd been beating Lawler's ass. He could have won. But he didn't win. When Lawler quit he took away Bert's chance to win.

As the day wore on, though, Bert began to realize he didn't feel all that bad. It was like he was supposed to be mad or sad or crushed or something. But he didn't feel any of those things. He just felt a little let down. He'd gone there to play a match, and he didn't get to play one because his opponent had been a poor sport. Bert had played great up to thirteen points, though, and he now knew beyond a doubt that Lawler was the prick he'd always thought he was. The morning hadn't been wasted. It was amazing: After all the time and all the work, Gary Lawler just didn't matter that much anymore. Bert looked forward to playing him again. Maybe he could shut him out.

When a guy came in looking for used Commando parts, Bert took him back to the shed and forgot all about Gary Lawler.

They didn't get to eat till after closing. Dave, who dealt with machines a lot more comfortably than with the motorcycling public, went home with a migraine. Bert and

Scotty sat in back with a bag of fishwiches and ignored all knocks on the door.

Scotty drained his Coke in one long pull, then burped. "So how'd your match come out?" he asked.

Bert grabbed a bottle out of the machine and tossed it to him. "I was up thirteen–five in the first game and he quit," Bert said.

"He quit?" Scotty said. "Was he hurt?"

"I served to his forehand and he called it a screen. It wasn't a screen and I told him so. He called me a foul-mouthed kid who didn't know the game, and he quit."

"Why, that chickenshit motherfucker," Scotty said. "But you know," he said, "it doesn't surprise me. Lawler played B for years. He stayed there so he could beat everybody. Now he runs into a real player and he fucking quits. That doesn't surprise me a bit."

"He said he'd play if we had a ref."

"Ref?" Scotty said. "Anybody who knows racquetball and knows that asshole too would disqualify him before he got on the court. It'd be a matter of respect for the game."

Bert smiled. "I think I can beat the guy."

"Beat him?" Scotty said. "Lawler wouldn't last three games with you if we locked him in the court."

Bert smiled. Now here was something that felt good. Having a Coke and a fishwich after work with Scotty. And feeling that he respected you. And feeling that he liked you. Beating Lawler three straight wouldn't feel as good as this.

Chapter 31

If Rock and Roll Were a Machine

Scotty had told Bert not to bring anything to the party except a pair of shorts for the hot tub. On the advice of his mother, however, Bert was bringing some eats and drinks. He'd bungeed a milk crate to his luggage rack, and in it he stowed a bag of Cheetos, two liters of Hire's root beer, and a jar of sliced jalapeños, along with his shorts and towel. Bert liked the milk-crate look. It was understated, functional, workmanly. And so was he. As long as you didn't count schoolwork.

Scotty and Rita lived northeast of town off Mt. Spokane State Park Road. Bert passed wheat and alfalfa fields where rows of young plants swayed in the spring breeze like eelgrass at the bottom of a stream, and he passed thick stands of pine and fir that cast the road in cool shadow. After the farms thinned out and the road began to climb, Bert caught sight of the big SHEPARD-DIXON mailbox and took the turn Scotty's directions—which Bert had taped to his gas tank—indicated.

Trees grew so thick along this lower road into the property that Bert was only able to see glimpses of the house on the cliff above. The slope steepened for a ways, then the trees thinned, then he was rolling onto the level concrete driveway lined with motorcycles.

Bert nosed the Norton between a 500 Triumph and an Ariel-sidecar rig and swung down the kickstand. A lot of the bikes belonged to people who visited the shop, and he recognized others from the club. He heard Rita's voice and looked up. She stood at the rail of the deck that ran from the house to a rock outcropping among the trees. "Come up through the garage, Bert," she said.

Bert stood for a minute. It was neat to see people walking around up there against a background of pine and fir boughs and blue sky. A kid four or five years old was sitting with his arms and legs stuck out between the railing supports straining to touch the end of a bough. He couldn't quite reach it.

On his way up the stairs Bert passed Camille's bedroom. Maps of the continents covered the two walls he could see from the doorway. Pinned between Europe and North America was a big green-and-gold Thompson High pennant. It surprised Bert and it touched him that a kid as sophisticated and accomplished as Camille would have a school pennant on his wall.

When he climbed another set of stairs and entered the kitchen Bert saw he was in a trailer. A mobile home. Or what had been a mobile home before most of one side had been removed and a house built around it. He also saw out the kitchen windows the cars parked up here on top of the cliff. He knew all these people couldn't have come on motorcycles. Rita took the Cheetos. "You kids and your Cheetos," she said. "The Cheetos company ought to put Jim Zimster on salary." She was wearing a baggy blue sweatshirt with cut-off sleeves. The gold letters on the front had about faded away. FBI ACADEMY, QUANTICO, VIRGINIA they said.

Rita took Bert's arm and led him through the big living room and out onto the deck. On the way Bert saw the guitars, amps, drums, piano, electronic keyboard, mikes, and other music stuff at the far end of the room. The prospect of live rock and roll was a thrill. And so was the prospect of a burger.

Scotty was at the grill and Zimster sat nearby cutting tomatoes and onions on a cutting board on his lap. Krista James and a college girl Bert recognized from aerobics were mashing hamburger patties at the picnic table. Krista said hi and Bert said hi. The college girl looked up and smiled. "Racquetball," she said. "Aerobics," Bert replied. "How ya doin'?" He set the root beer and peppers on the table.

Scotty handed Bert the spatula. "Hope you don't mind working on your day off," he said. Bert smiled, and Scotty was off into the house. Bert looked down. The burgers and hot dogs on the grill were just starting to sizzle. He felt a pull on the leg of his jeans. It was the little boy who'd been reaching out for the tree. Another boy and a girl stood at his sides. He held a tiny green pine cone in his hand.

"We're hungry," the little guy said.

Bert looked down at the three. "Dogs or burgers?"

"Hot dogs!" his pals shouted.

"Burgers!" the kid screamed.

They tried to outshout one another.

Bert menaced them with the spatula until they were quiet. "Okay," he said. "You guys get the first ones when they're cooked."

The three threw up their arms, screamed, and began banging into one another like tiny wide receivers after a long TD pass. They whirled away, but the one kid circled back and approached the grill. He stood on his tiptoes and peered down into the coals. Then he tossed in his pine cone. It sizzled for a second. The sound was audible above the sizzling meat. Then it burst into flame and was gone. There was nothing left. The boy looked up at Bert with a conspirator's smile, then dodged off through the forest of legs.

Scotty had returned by the time the meat was getting close. Bert hunted up the kids and brought them back to be the first ones served.

It was fun to serve with Scotty. All they did was put burgers and dogs on buns for people, but it was fun to be there with him and to be of use. Bert knew a lot of the guests and greeted someone by name. It was funny that such a simple thing as calling a person by name felt good. But it did. A lot of men and women from the leagues and from team racquetball were there. Bert allowed himself to take pleasure that Gary Lawler was not among them.

* * *

Bert, Jim, Krista, and Mike Jackson ate on the floor in front of the instruments so they'd have good seats when the music started. Camille and Rita were distributing ear protection—the earmuff kind that shooters use— to the little kids, and Bert overheard Rita tell a woman with a baby that this would be a good time for her to walk down the trail and spend some time in the hot tub. The woman said she wanted to hear the guys play, and Rita told her not to worry, that people for miles around would hear them.

Bert turned and looked at the amps. They were old and scuffed, but they were big. A tall amp stood in each corner, and on top of the tall amp sat a smaller one. The stacks reached nearly to the ceiling. The name on them was MARSHALL. They looked like they could produce some heavy decibels. Some serious sound.

Bert was surprised to see Steve settle onto the stool behind the half-circle of drums. He wondered if there was anything the Shepards couldn't do.

Camille had his guitar strapped on, and Scotty was picking up a bass when the pine-cone kid, his pals, and Dave's two little girls wriggled their way up front. Scotty asked Willa and Sara where their ear protection was, and they pulled back their long brown hair and showed him the twisted hunks of toilet paper in their ears. Camille gave his dad a look of apology and said they'd run out of the shooters' earmuffs. "You kids sit right up by us,"

Scotty told them. "The loudest place is back there where your folks are."

Bert turned and saw Dave and his wife, Verna, sitting on the raised fireplace hearth at the far end of the room.

"Dave!" Scotty hollered. "Put your sunglasses on!"

As Dave reached into his shirt pocket, Scotty, Steve, and Camille turned and reached to the floor. When they faced the room again they were Billy Gibbons look-alikes: sunglasses, shoulder-length hair, beards to their belly buttons. They looked just like Dave.

Verna covered her face with her hands. Dave shook his head, the rest of the guests hooted, and Steve banged out those first drumbeats of "Sleeping Bag."

At first Bert was fascinated by the idea that these guys he knew could do this amazing thing. Then he was swept up in the thing itself, the rock and roll, the controlled explosion of sound that pulled you to it as it knocked you back, that drove you like a piston and took you for a ride.

Then when Camille took his guitar break, a part of the ride that Bert had been on since back in September ended. This guy played guitar with a greater ease than Bert breathed. Here was the gift exposed in its fullness, and it was so far beyond Bert's imaginings of himself that he couldn't even envy it.

Then Bert saw that look pass between Camille and Scotty again. It was different than on the football field. Then Camille had been looking up, and his expression contained a quality of aspiration. Now he was on the same level as his father, and both their expressions suggested a long journey ended and a destination attained. The beards they wore didn't cover this. Their sunglasses didn't hide it. Bert saw it all over them.

Everyone clapped and yelled when the song ended. The Shepards took off their glasses, false hair, and beards and smiled. The pine-cone kid grabbed the stuff from Camille and put it on. The beard reached to his tennies.

The kid accompanied Camille on air guitar through Bob Seger's "Her Strut," "Fire Lake," and "Roll It Away." Bert watched the little guy and understood what it was that Lawler had taken from him back in fifth and sixth grades. It was part of his childhood. It was the quality in healthy kids that allows them to act without self-consciousness, that allows them to develop a sense of who they are before they start caring so much about what the world thinks of them. This is what was taken, and Bert knew it was gone forever. But he also knew that much abided, as Tanneran's quote said. He wasn't empty. He was full. He just wished he could give a name to the fullness.

The Shepards played for a long time, then took a break, then they played a long time again. Scotty and Camille traded around on guitar and keyboard. They played some great tunes Bert knew and some he was hearing for the first time: George Thorogood's "Bad to the Bone," Eric Clapton's "Old Love" and "Running on Faith" from the

Journeyman CD and "Sunshine of Your Love" and "Badge" from his Cream days, the Eagles' "Life in the Fast Lane," John Cougar Mellencamp's "Cherry Bomb" and "Shama Lama Ding Dong," Leon Russell's "Tightrope."

The sun had fallen below the trees by the time they finally gave it up. The light flooding in from the deck was tinged with the blue of dusk, and the air was moist and cool. Bert saw the pine-cone kid being carried out asleep on his father's shoulder.

Bert thanked Camille, Steve, then Scotty for the great music and the great day. "It's not over yet," Scotty said. "We've gotta take a soak in the tub."

"Club closes early tonight," Bert replied. "I've got to hustle to make it. I didn't realize things would go this long." He had his workout bag packed and sitting on the porch at Gram's.

"Next time, then," Scotty said. "I'll walk ya out."

"Next time," Bert said.

They stood beside Bert's Norton. "It's all coming down to the end," Scotty said. "You never think it'll come, but then you look up and see it's all about over.

"I left my wife and son sixteen years ago," Scotty said. "But Camille grew up a happy kid, his mom is a hell of a lot better off, and Rita and I have a sweet life here. Seems like it all worked out for the best. But you know something, Bert?"

Bert kept his eyes on Scotty's face.

"I haven't forgotten an ounce of the heartache I caused

or the heartache I felt. I still feel it. People think the past goes away, but it doesn't. Not the stuff done to us or the stuff we do to others. A guy carries that shit on his back forever. We can get strong enough so it carries easier," Scotty said. "But we carry it till we die."

Bert knew Scotty was talking about himself, but it felt like he was talking about Bert's life too. But how could he be? How could Scotty know?

"You're strong, Bert," Scotty said. "You've got strength and you've got desire. Look at you now. You make a deal with yourself to go work out, and that's what you by God do." Scotty tapped him on the shoulder with the side of his fist. "Go get 'em," he said.

Bert rode his Norton through the cool blue shadows toward the golden streaks of setting sun. So there was the name for what abides: strength. Strength and desire. What more could a guy need? What more could he ask for?

I could be a rock-and-roller, Bert said to himself. I could be a guitar hero. But chances are I won't. He smiled into the wind. But if rock and roll were a machine, it would be a motorcycle, he said. And I've got one of those.

He turned his throttle and the volume rose. He lost himself in the music.

Turn the page for a peek at
Terry Davis's cult classic,
Vision Quest.

Both Dad and I are pretty sure Shute is going to grind my body into the green surface of our David Thompson High School wrestling mat. We work hard to put that thought out of our minds, though. I don't wrestle Shute until after the first of the year, when the weights come up two pounds and I move down from the 154-pound class— where I'm already lean—to become probably the world's hungriest 147-pounder. I've got two weeks yet. We also put it out of our minds because today is my birthday and Dad had our 1941 DeSoto reupholstered in the original mohair. He presented it to me this morning in celebration of my eighteen years and my upcoming high school graduation. Still, he couldn't forget my impending doom. After he caressed the leather armrests, rubbed up the bristling new fabric, and spun the big old steering wheel with one finger, he noted that Carla will be able to drive me around in style and solid comfort after Shute breaks all my bones. Carla is my girl friend. She lives with us.

Carla loves the DeSoto. Today we eat our lunch in it, and she spreads a red-and-white checkered tablecloth over the backseat so she won't drip yogurt on the mohair. I sit in front, manning our Sony portable cassette recorder, playing a Beatles collection and the Stones' "Hot Rocks," eating raw carrots and celery and hard-boiled eggs, turning to pure protein before her very eyes as she hands me another carrot. I'm down to 150.

Carla climbs in front and rubs the dash and window moldings with a waxed cloth Dad brought her from the store.

Dad's in the car business. People in the car business call their places "stores" now. The name has gone through phases. When I was a little kid playing park league baseball Dad would say he was going to the "garage." And when I was in junior high playing Pop Warner football he'd say he was going to the "lot." But now it's "store."

I see Belle walking our way as I finally open the car door to head for my English class. The wind blows hard and for a second my eyes hurt from the cold. "Hi, folksies!" yells Belle, slipping and nearly falling on the icy sidewalk. Belle, you crack, don't do any dope in our car, I think to myself, nodding to her.

Belle is the gum-freeze queen of David Thompson High and Carla's best friend after me. She's wrecked a good share of the time, especially at school. She's usually holding dope and I would would hate to see her nabbed for it with Carla. It seems that most of the administration and teachers and kids take Belle's space travel for the effervescence of school spirit. I suppose it's because she's a cheerleader and beautiful. There's really not much chance of her getting caught around school, but I still worry.

Belle is friendly and funny and a good person. She's never done me wrong. The chance of her getting Carla in trouble is the only thing I don't like about Belle. I sound like a parent. Carla wouldn't like it if she knew I felt this way. There's probably nothing to worry about. Carla is pretty down on chemicals and kind of down on dope in general, and she's afraid Belle is overdoing it. I doubt Carla would allow Belle to do any dope in her presence.

I'm smiling big and thinking about friendship as Carla waves good-bye with her waxed cloth. I'm also being careful not to fall on my ass. If I'm going to have my coccyx broken, I'd rather Shute did it than this transient and impersonal patch of ice.

Coach Ratta passes me in the gym door. "What do you weigh?" he asks.

"Fifty," I reply, stopping for a bit. We always leave out the one hundred.

His eyebrows rise. "Can you beat Kuchera?" he asks, eyebrows coming down. He knows I can. What he doubts is that I can make 147 without losing my strength.

"Yes," I reply, thinking how much I like Kuch and how badly I can munch his body, and wishing we didn't have to wrestle off for the spot, but not wishing it too hard because it will only be for this one match.

"We'll see," Coach Ratta says. He's sure I'm losing my strength.

Coach and most of the team and a lot of other people at school were pretty pissed off at me for deciding to graduate a semester early. I'll miss a couple league matches and the district and state tournaments. But Doug Bowden, our number-two guy at 154, is undefeated in his junior varsity matches and is going to put a lot of varsity guys on their backs once he gets the chance. I thought about this before I made my decision.

Coach isn't mad anymore and neither is anybody on the team. Dad figured from the start it was okay as long as I was sure. And Carla thought it was a good idea, especially since I'd be working full-time and earning money to help Dad. It worries my mom a little, but that's her nature.

Senior English is a nice class. We read novels and short stories and we write essays and discuss. Gene Tanneran, our teacher, says we must articulate with both pen and tongue, so he grades us on class participation.

Gene continually tries to bring up his two favorite subjects for ridicule, Richard Nixon and Spiro Agnew. I figure the two sonsabitches aren't worth my time. Gene and Thurston Reilly, who is editor of the school paper and wants to be a muckraking columnist, get the biggest kick out of Nixon's "Checkers" speech, in which the big dick swears that the guys who contributed to his slush fund never asked him for any special favors, points out his sweet wife's respectable Republican cloth coat, and vows ardently never to return

Checkers, the lovable cocker sent to him by a Texan who must have been a real dog-hater.

Gene shows the film once a month and he and Thurston just howl. I thought it was funny the first time, but now I think it's sad. The way I see it, if people ever saw or heard that speech and were still dumb or evil enough to vote for the bastard, they deserve everything he'll ever do to them.

Gene's also got a record of Agnew's speeches. He figures Agnew should be public enemy number one for making parents hate and fear their own children. Gene loved it when I told him my dad thinks I'm a pretty good guy and Agnew is a flaming asshole.

Tanneran wrestled in high school and college. He asks me what I weigh as we walk out of class.

"I'm down to fifty," I say.

"Fat city!" Gene exclaims, savoring the irony. "You're gonna make it!"

We hold our wrestle-offs after our regular practice. That's *after* two hours of exercises, running, takedowns, escapes, reversals, counters, pins, and getting-off-your-back drills. And a pin in a wrestle-off doesn't end the match. The guy who pins gets five points and you keep on going. I'm glad we do it this way. It really gets us in shape. Shute's chances of killing me would be even better if we didn't.

I've avoided Kuch all practice. Otto Lafte tied me to the trampoline as usual on wrestle-off days. We bounce around and wrestle on the trampoline and he always manages to get me on my stomach and then he sits on my back. Once he gets me down it's all over. Otto weighs 243. He stretches the leg straps of my jock around my ankles; then he hooks the waistband through the tramp springs. I think it calms him somehow. Wrestle-offs shouldn't bother Otto—he's been David Thompson's number-one heavyweight for two and a half years. Kuch usually participates in the trampoline ritual. Not that Otto needs the help. It's just something we do. Sometimes Otto and I get Kuch. Sometimes Kuch and I and Balldozer get Otto.

Sometimes we pluck the guy's pubic hair. Little Jerry Konigi is plucked almost bald. He weighs ninety eight pounds. Everybody takes out their frustrations on Jerry.

Coach Ratta untied me. Then as I jumped down from the tramp he caught me midair and drove me to the mat. He does this all the time. I think he got the idea from Peter Seller's valet, Kato, the guy who's always sneaking up and attacking him in the Pink Panther movies. Coach says he does it to keep us constantly alert when we're on the mat, and especially when we're in a match and one wrestler has just escaped and gotten to his feet. A lot of guys get taken down at that point in a match. If you're the one who's escaped, you have this tendency to relax, because you've just gotten out of a hold and scored yourself a point—and you leave yourself open to getting taken right back to the mat. And if you're the one who's let the other guy escape, you have this tendency to say shit and shake your head and relax for a second—and then the guy takes you down and gets two more points on you. He let me up without saying a word and turned toward the door to the main wrestling room. I untied my sweat pants and had my eyes on my crotch as I adjusted my jock when he knocked me down again. This time he took me right to my back. I was pinned before I could get my hands out of my pants. I guess Coach doesn't want me getting overconfident.

Not only do we hold our wrestle-offs after a full

practice, but we wrestle nine minutes instead of the regular six. And even if you pin or get pinned, you still have to go the full nine.

Kuch is ready. He's spoken with the Everywhere Spirit and now he's shouting his war cries. He took a lot of shit about his Indian stuff from crowds last season, especially on the road. People wrote the principal and called him on the phone to complain about Kuch's aboriginal behavior on the mat. Kuch doesn't consult with the Everywhere Spirit in public anymore and the only time he uses his war cry is at the whistle when he's on the bottom in the referee's position. But he still does all his Indian stuff when he wrestles off.

Kuch screams and I bounce in my takedown dance. I'm too fast. I take him down with single-leg dives, double-leg dives, sweeps. I counter his dives with a whizzer, slipping my arm under his armpit to the back of his head and levering downward so he either has to let go of my leg or get flipped over on his back. Kuch is strong. If he locks me up he can snap my head down to the mat or shuck me off, spinning me sideways, opening me up for a fireman's carry. I dance away and don't lock up with Kuch. We go takedowns for three minutes and I lead 12–0.

Now we go to the referee's position—one guy down on his hands and knees and the other guy kneeling beside him with one arm around his waist, fingers on his belly button, and the other hand gripping his elbow. The top guys's chin is in line with the bottom guy's spine. They both look straight ahead at the referee's hand, which is supposed to move at the same time he blows his whistle to start the round. The down guy has the better chance to score points. He can escape for one point, or reverse and get control of the top guy for two points. The top guy tries to keep control and work for a pin. In a real match, when you escape you work for a takedown, and when you reverse you work for a pin. But in wrestle-offs, when we get an escape or a reversal we go back to the referee's position and start again.

Kuch is down first. He's very strong and he's quick. He pops right to his feet, screaming, trying for an escape. But I go to a double-heel trip and haul him back down to the mat. He's too out of breath now to keep up his steady stream of war cries. I counter his sitout. I follow him on his roll. I try to pin him toward the end of the round, but either I'm too tired or he's not tired enough. I can't take him to his back.

Now I get three minutes from down. I throw my best moves from here. I walk out on him—"crawl" out, actually, charging on my hands and knees, like a giant little kid escaping from his playpen; then I explode into a sitout and reverse for two points. I pop to my feet, bellowing like a goosed dromedary, and use a standing switch for two. I lock his arm and roll, escaping for a point. I buck back and hip over, reversing for two. I throw an outside switch and lean back hard for leverage on the arm Kuch is trying to hold me with. I'm levering hard and have almost worked behind him to gain control when he lets me go and pulls his arm away. I fall flat on my back. He's on me in half a breath and I'm pinned. Renewed, he whoops and dances and kicks me in the ass a few times, smiling. We go back to the referee's position and wait for Coach's whistle.

"Funny, smart, tough."

—Chris Crutcher, Margaret A. Edwards Award–winning author

RATS SAW GOD

BY ROB THOMAS

CREATOR OF *VERONICA MARS*

everything doesn't have to make sense.

★"[A] beautifully crafted, emotionally charged story....
[S]o hip and cool and strong it hurts."—*SLJ*, starred review

PRINT AND EBOOK EDITIONS AVAILABLE

SIMON & SCHUSTER BFYR

TEEN.SimonandSchuster.com

RYAN DEAN GRAPPLES WITH LIFE, LOVE, AND RUGBY.

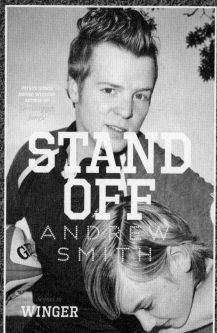

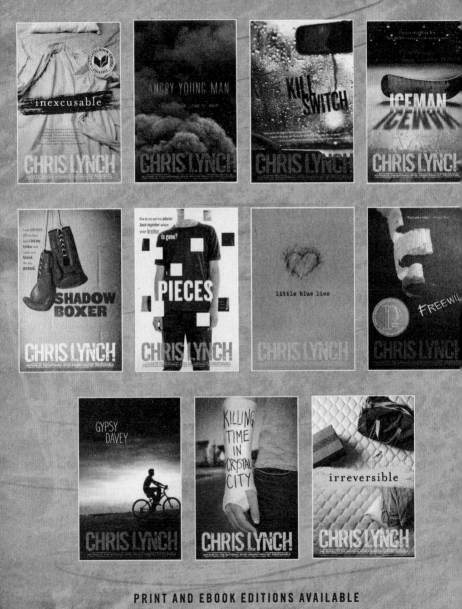

WHEN YOU'RE LIVING A LIE,
THE TRUTH CAN SET YOU FREE . . .
OR COST YOU YOUR LIFE.

DANGEROUS
LIES

NEW YORK TIMES BESTSELLING AUTHOR

BECCA
FITZPATRICK